Small
World

Small World

A MAH JONGG TABLE TALK TALE

Karen Gooen

Author of *Searching for Bubbe Fischer*

BUBBE MEISES PUBLISHERS

For permission requests, contact the author via email: bubbefischer@gmail.com.

ISBN: 978-0-9907601-1-5 (paperback book)
978-0-9907601-0-8 (ebook)

Cover and book design by Duane Stapp

Printed in the United States of America

First Printing 2016

In honor of mahj players everywhere
and in memory of Sharon Kasmanoff,
I offer this celebration of friendship.

Small World

Prologue

"I had to see it with my own eyes," my mother said. "I heard that Lois Benson was carrying on last Monday, but I didn't believe it would come to this!"

She had called me for our usual late-morning phone chat, but the agitation in her voice was unnatural.

"What happened, Mom?" I asked.

"It was eerie, Talia. I was over at the Clubhouse this morning for my Zumba class. When it ended at 10:15, I dropped by the card room, and it was *deserted!*"

As in many retirement communities, the Clubhouse in my mother's neighborhood is the hub of social activity, and the card room is ground zero. Various constituencies have control of the room each day from ten until two: they have "Monday Morning Mahj" and its Thursday counterpart, Canasta on Tuesdays and Fridays, and poker on Wednesdays and Saturdays. Bingo begins at noon on Sundays.

"Today's Thursday, so it should be a mah jongg day, right?" I asked.

"That's what I thought, too," she said. "I poked my head in to say hello, and I felt like I was looking at a saloon in some abandoned ghost town. The tables were arranged, there were even pitchers of water. It was all set up for people to come and play, but nobody was there. Not one person, on a Thursday morning. It was very strange."

She continued, "Harriet Freiman told me that Lois Benson threw a fit at the last Monday Morning Mahj, but I didn't think she'd scare *everyone* away." She paused, still trying to comprehend what she'd seen. "The room was empty!"

I waited for her to say more. Mom loved sharing stories about the goings-on in her little neighborhood, Parnassus Pines. It was only ten minutes away from my house in northern New Jersey. She particularly enjoyed talking about situations like this one, where she wasn't personally affected. We figured that it wasn't really gossiping. It was more like a news program—or an ongoing soap opera.

"Wait a second. Passover starts tomorrow night. People have to cook and clean and get ready, don't they?" I asked.

"That's no excuse. Half of the ladies who play mah jongg here aren't even Jewish!" she replied.

"So what happened on Monday? What exactly did Lois Benson do?" I asked.

Mom sighed. I could picture her, shaking her head in disbelief. "Harriet told me that she and some of the other ladies showed up at the card room a few minutes early Monday morning, so there were already two full tables playing by the time Lois Benson arrived. Lois went over to observe them and pointed out that they were still using the 2011 card."

I nodded as I listened. The National Mah Jongg League creates a list of new hands every year. It's a multicolored, trifold document that includes about sixty hands that all NMJL players pursue and attempt to achieve for the next twelve months. The League sends it out in late March or early April. Today was April fifth.

"But Monday was only the second day of April!" I exclaimed, with some annoyance. "Give me a break!"

"I know!" my mother replied, matching my indignation.

"But there was Lois, complaining that Harriet and her group weren't using the 2012 card. The mail doesn't even *come* on Sunday! Davida Roth was sitting at Harriet's table and said that even though she had her new card, not everyone had theirs yet, and it wasn't fair to leave some people out. Davida said that they should switch to the new card after April fifteenth, when all the players had received theirs."

"That sounds perfectly reasonable to me," I said.

"Apparently, Lois just exploded," my mother said. "She told the ladies at the table that they were playing illegally, and that no one should be allowed to play with the old card after March thirty-first."

"Has Lois appointed herself the mahj police, or something?" I asked.

"I think she's got a screw loose," my mother said. "But yes, she does think she runs mah jongg here. She's taught the beginners' class for almost six years, and she comes to the Clubhouse drop-ins every Monday and Thursday and tries to impose her will on everyone. She also organizes two tournaments, in February and August."

"You've mentioned those," I said.

"Funny thing about those tournaments—she claims that they're fundraisers, but no one ever hears about there being a specific charity." Her voice was laden with innuendo. "I wonder…"

"Still, not everyone in the neighborhood has to do what she says," I argued. "Just because she's active doesn't make her the Mah Jongg Queen of Parnassus Pines. *You* don't play with her."

"No," my mother agreed, "I avoid her like the plague. She's overbearing and obnoxious. Harriet and Davida go to the drop-in days, and to her tournaments, because they don't have to travel at all. Lots of people do, because it's just convenient. I refuse. I don't want to have anything to do with her."

I had to laugh. It was absurd to think that there was a Mah Jongg Mussolini dictating how the game must be played in this small senior community. "Why does she care what's going on at the other tables in the Clubhouse? It all sounds crazy!"

"That's the thing," my mother said. "Just because *she* doesn't want to play with the old card doesn't mean that she can make everyone else conform. As other groups came in and started playing, she would wander over and see what they were up to. She kept on yelling at people, and finally she stood at the door, saying, 'You can't come in without the new card! No more using the 2011 card!' She really upset some people."

"And Harriet and Davida stuck around all day, just to watch this?" I asked. "I can't imagine that anyone has *that* much free time."

"No, they gave up and went home after about twenty minutes, but Harriet heard from other people who experienced the same thing. There were a few ladies who had brought the new card and they were allowed to play. One of them told Harriet that Lois stayed there, guarding the doorway, until almost two o'clock."

I tried to picture this seventy-year-old Mah Jongg Monitor, blocking the door and inspecting people's mah jongg cards like a bouncer at some nightclub. Although I'd only met Lois Benson once or twice, she had created quite an impression. She had close-cropped, auburn-dyed hair that sometimes looked purple, but otherwise had a pale complexion and wore little makeup except for her penciled-in auburn brows. She was tall and solidly built, and came across as officious and altogether formidable. It didn't surprise me that she'd intimidated some of the quieter women, like Harriet, but I was pleased to see that Davida had stood up to her.

I heard the click of call waiting from my mother's end of the line. "Hold on, Talia, I've got another call," she told me.

After two minutes, she came back on. "That was Harriet. She said Lois sent out an email to all the regulars: 'No one is allowed to play in the Clubhouse unless they use the current NMJL card,' so Davida sent out a counter-email: 'Per the above, out of respect for all Parnassus Pines residents, we are suspending Clubhouse play until April sixteenth. Feel free to play in private homes until that time, using whatever card you wish.' Harriet says that nine of them are over at Davida's house, playing the 2011 card, right now.

"I hate to see something like this tearing the community apart," she added. "We're going to have to do something about Lois Benson. I'm going over to Davida's, and then I have to make some more phone calls."

"Keep me posted," I said. "I know how these ladies love their mahj."

———

I should have known that my mother, Frances "Franny" Klein, Second Vice President of the Parnassus Pines Community Association, would straighten things out. The next afternoon, when she came over to help me prepare for our Passover seder, she gave me the lowdown:

"The Executive Committee had an emergency session this morning. They're firing Lois Benson. They have decided that the Clubhouse mah jongg class will be led by a nonresident from now on, to avoid any personal conflicts within the Pines community. Since they didn't say anything about nepotism, I recommended you for the position. Your interview is in two weeks."

Spring

"It's important to keep the game moving," I said to my beginners' class, a dozen ladies sitting around a large table. "Remember: it's not brain surgery, don't overthink each decision. No one's going to die if you throw the wrong tile!"

No response. If I'd been using a microphone, I would have tapped it, asking, "Is this thing on?"

I've been teaching mah jongg for a couple of years now, ever since the "New Card Fiasco of 2012," otherwise known as Lois Benson's meltdown. I've had some gossipy groups that were more interested in socializing than learning the tiles, and I've had some repeat customers who never managed to grasp the main concepts, but the group in front of me was my toughest one to date: I simply couldn't get a reaction out of them.

There's no doubt that the material is challenging. The game is complicated, and requires some concentration and focus in order to learn properly. I'd found these ladies to be excellent students, paying close attention and dutifully taking notes, but they just weren't warming up or interacting with one another. They weren't *having fun*. Half of the objective is to socialize and make friends, and hopefully get some emotional fulfillment out of playing, whether you win or lose. But how can any of that happen, if you're surrounded by robots?

"Okay, then. I'm going to take a five-minute break, maybe you want to stretch your legs?" I asked. Still no reaction.

The whiteboard was covered in green and red ink. It showed my illustrations of certain hands and examples of when a joker could and couldn't be used. I started erasing the board and looked up to see one of my students, Becky, waiting patiently for me to finish.

Becky, like most of her classmates, had lived in Parnassus Pines for several years. As usual, the group only included women. In my two-plus years of teaching, I've only had one male student, who took the class with his wife. The ladies in this group ranged in age from their middle fifties to early seventies. About half were married, three or four were widows, and one was a divorcée. They were retired schoolteachers, secretaries, salespeople, or medical assistants, and generally what I call "white ethnic": Jewish, Irish, Italian, Polish, or Greek. Parnassus Pines was not a very racially diverse neighborhood.

Becky seemed friendlier than most of the other ladies in this group. At least she made an attempt at small talk.

"I used to work for a brain surgeon," she said. "He was very absentminded, kept losing things."

I laughed. "Sometimes I say, 'It's not rocket science.' One of these days, I'll be teaching a former NASA employee, and then I'll have to come up with another expression."

"You're trying to get them to loosen up," Becky reasoned.

"I wish it would work. I mean, I'm all for taking it seriously—I want to learn the game because everybody around here plays—but I was hoping to make a few new friends in this class."

"Do you have any idea why no one cracks a smile?" I asked. "Is it me? Am I too strict?"

"I don't think so. I've had that same problem with Gail for years. She's the one over there in the gray cardigan. She lives two doors down from me. I used to invite her over, but she never came, and she doesn't acknowledge me when I see her at the grocery store. I've stopped trying to get personal. She barely even responds to 'Hi, nice weather we're having,' or 'Did you read the notice about repaving the sidewalk this week?'"

"I appreciate that comment about your boss," I said to her. "At least I know that someone's listening." Then, to the group at large, I said, "Okay, come on back. I'm going to split you into tables of four now!"

Over these two class sessions, I had watched how some players gravitated to one another, even if just as pairs, and decided that I would put the "lone wolves" together at one table. Becky was part of this group, along with three others: Cheryl, Leslie, and Martha.

As I helped them set up their tiles, I watched the ladies relax a little bit. I had moved their table away from the other two, so that they wouldn't feel constrained to limit their conversation.

Quite intentionally, I started laying the groundwork for turning their group into a socially supportive environment. I sighed as I began stacking the tiles, and made up a story. "It's really been a tough month for me," I confessed. "My son, Benjy, handled all of his college applications, and even did his on-site visits by himself. He doesn't want to talk about his admissions decisions, and they'll be coming any day now. I'm not ready for him to be so independent. He's my baby!"

A personal revelation! Of course, part of it was true—I wasn't ready for Benjy to be so independent, and he'd told me that he would let me know if or when he was ready to talk—but I made it sound like it was unexpectedly troubling, when in fact it was how Benjy *always* behaved.

My maternal lament sparked a sympathetic reaction from the students.

Martha said, "That's a shame. It's always tough when they're getting ready to move on. They become very rude and selfish for a while. What do they call it, 'fouling the nest'?" The other ladies nodded.

"I remember my youngest daughter's senior year of high school. She couldn't wait to leave!" said Cheryl. "She found a job on campus during her freshman year and only came home twice that entire summer! I was heartbroken. I guess some kids are just ready."

"Oh, where did your daughter go to school?" asked Leslie.

"Rutgers Business School," said Cheryl. "Class of 2010."

"Ah, my niece was Rutgers Class of 2011. School of Pharmacy. What was your daughter's major?" asked Martha.

"Marketing. Now she has a job with a home goods chain. She's working on their advertising."

"Does she get to write the jingles?" asked Becky.

And they were off. I made sure they remembered how to do the passing. I would murmur, "Put three together that you know you don't need...those are going across..." but meanwhile, the ladies were sharing stories. They were even laughing. Loudly.

The players at the other two tables looked up for a moment to see what the commotion was about. I moved away from my no-longer "lone" wolves. My work there was done. "Let's focus on what to pass," I said to the second group, which included Gail. She had craned her neck to see what was going on at Becky's table. "Look at the tiles. What patterns do you see? Are there more evens, or odds, or maybe they're all at one end of the number line?" I asked her.

I wanted to see my players get better, but I also wanted them to have a good time. That meant they'd keep playing the game and, hopefully, would recommend me to their friends. It was important that I keep up my enrollment, in order to please the Board at Parnassus Pines and keep Lois Benson at bay. My mom assured me that even if I was terrible, the Board was never going to hire her back. They didn't want to stir up the same problems again.

My mother had been eager to curb Lois's power, but she also had *my* best interests at heart when she recommended me for the teaching position. As soon as she heard there was an opening, she recognized that it was the right career move for me.

This was especially helpful since, at that point, I *had* no career. My daughter Abby was in college at the time, and Benjy was a sophomore in high school. Mom saw the writing on the wall before I did: "Empty nest approaching... must find meaningful occupation." And she was right.

It turns out I'm a natural fit for teaching, because I love the game and want to share it with other players. Besides Parnassus Pines, I've taught at several other local senior residential complexes and retirement villages. It's certainly not a high-paying gig, but I get a lot of satisfaction from it in two ways:

I enjoy helping students grasp the concepts. I love watching the reaction when a player wins for the first time. She finds that the pieces literally click into place. The whole premise of the game suddenly makes sense to her. At the same time, she gets a rush of endorphins from her victory and realizes that she wants to keep winning on her own.

I also like helping students make personal connections. Although it's a challenging game, there's enough down time between hands for conversation. These ladies make friends, or at least acquaintances that can blossom into friendship over a few years' time. I love to help people make connections. I'm setting up the kindling—a foursome like Becky, Cheryl, Leslie, and Martha—and lighting a spark. It's their responsibility to keep the fire going.

When class ended, I left the Clubhouse and stopped by my mother's unit to say hello. I didn't always have time to see her and thought it would be a nice surprise.

Her Ford Taurus was in the driveway, but when I knocked on her front door, there was no answer. I called her cell phone and it immediately went to voice mail.

"Hi, Mom. I'm standing on your doorstep. It's about 2:30 and you're nowhere to be found. Call me later, okay?"

I tried to remember. Had we even spoken today? I realized I'd headed out to run some errands and then went straight to class, and never picked up the phone to call.

I was still standing at her front door, feeling the early-spring chill. I dialed her house phone, worried that she might be somewhere inside, unable to get to the phone. Those TV commercials for emergency alerts were effective; I imagined Mom groaning on the floor by her bathtub. Although she was only seventy-four, she was as prone to falling as anyone, and she *did* live alone. After four rings, I again got her voice mail.

I reached deep into my purse for the emergency key. I seldom used it; this wasn't the house I grew up in, after all, so I never thought of it as "home," and I hated to just barge in. At that moment, however, my fears overwhelmed my sense of decorum. I unlocked the door and flung it open.

"Mom? Mom, are you here? Are you okay?"

I rushed through the front foyer area, past the kitchen, and straight back to her bedroom and the master bath. I was surprised to find...nothing. She was nowhere to be found, which was concerning, but at least she wasn't slumped over in a heap on the bathroom floor.

I went back to the kitchen and jotted down a note. "Came by after class, but you weren't around. Give me a call—T."

I stuck around the house for a few minutes, looking at old photographs and souvenirs. I glanced at my mother and father's wedding pictures, taken back in 1962 when they were fresh out of college. My mother looked beautiful in her wedding gown. They both looked so innocent and full of hope.

Their story was bittersweet. She met my father at a summer camp in the Adirondacks when she was eighteen. He was a senior counselor for twelve-year-old boys, and she was the junior archery instructor. I'm sure that their friends made plenty of "she shot him with an arrow" Cupid jokes at the time.

They dated for a few years and got married right after her graduation from Hunter. They lived in the City for a while. She taught elementary school while he finished Fordham Law School, and then they moved out to the New Jersey suburbs so she could devote herself to raising me and my brother, Steven.

The original idea was that Dad would become a partner in a big, important law firm, and Mom would never have to work outside the home. She would focus on helping her adorable children grow up healthy and strong, and one day we would provide them with lots of even more adorable grandchildren. Then Mom and Dad would live out their retirement days in Boca Raton.

Everything was going beautifully, according to plan, but there is some truth to the Yiddish saying: *"Mann tracht, Gott lacht."* Man plans, God laughs. Some of those things did happen, but not all. And not always quite according to plan. Dad hadn't figured on the economic downturn during the late 1970s or on Mom being so bored at home that she'd *want* to go back to work. And none of us expected that Dad would suffer a fatal heart attack at age forty-four.

The good news was that Mom was left with a life insurance policy which covered the last of the mortgage, thereby keeping a roof over our heads. Unfortunately, among the other investments that Dad made, many (at the time) weren't doing very well. Steven and I were still in our teens, and Mom insisted that we had to go to the best colleges we could, that price was no object. She took out student loans and was adamant about paying them off herself. Fortunately, she was able to get a job as a primary grade teacher at a Jewish Day School.

When Mom retired in 2005, she just didn't have the heart to move down to Florida by herself. Instead she moved to Parnassus Pines, the "Perfect Development for Active Seniors" in our town. She kept busy with the usual activities: card games, gym classes, day trips, fundraisers. We spoke every day, and she seemed in good health, but this afternoon had really scared me. I hadn't thought of her not being around—I was about to lose Benjy to college, but it hadn't occurred to me that I might lose my mom too.

I checked the mail when I got home: two envelopes addressed to Benjy, one thick and one thin, both from Pace University. I figured the thick one was good news, but he had assured me that he'd tell me when there was something worth knowing. I ran upstairs to his room and left the two letters on his bed, then headed back downstairs to the laundry room. I wanted to immerse myself in chores for a while, rather than think about phones that weren't ringing or what those letters might mean.

At around 5 o'clock—finally—the phone rang. It was my mother checking in with me. I resisted the urge to scold her or guilt her with my worries. I attempted to sound cool and breezy.

"So you've been a busy girl, today," I said. "I didn't know you'd be out."

"Yes, I saw that you even came in the house. Are you all right?" she asked. "You don't usually check up on me like that."

"I'm fine," I said. "I just thought you'd be around, that's all. I happened to be at the Pines, teaching."

"That's right. The new class has begun. Everything's okay with me. I'm sorry I didn't get a chance to see you."

"Would you like to come over for dinner on Saturday?" I asked. "I can make something good."

"Um, not this week. They're showing *An Affair to Remember* at the Clubhouse. Maybe another time."

"Okay. We're still getting together for lunch on Thursday, right?" I asked.

"I don't think so. I've got a lot to do this week. I have to get ready for Book Club and I'm hosting Canasta."

"Canasta? You traitor!!" I joked. "How can you play anything but mah jongg?"

"Phyllis has her sister coming in for the week, and she wants to play, so there you go."

"Hmm," I said aloud. "How's Harriet settling in?"

"She loves it there. She's about five minutes from her daughter and sees the grandchildren twice a week." Harriet Freiman had moved out to Denver back in October to be closer to her daughter. I had been worried about Mom being lonely without her.

"Did they get a lot of snow this winter?" I asked.

"Not as much as New Jersey," she said. "It's actually a drier climate."

"Wow!" I said. "I had no idea."

My mother—my good-natured, doting mother—sighed, somewhat impatiently. "Talia, honey, I've got to take care of some things. I'll talk to you soon."

"Okay, Mom," I said. "Talk to you later. Love you."

It wasn't like my mother to be so preoccupied…or occupied. I knew she was a community leader, and had lots of friends in the development, but she always had time to chat with me. Every day. I suddenly felt abandoned, pushed off to the side because she had more important things to do.

———

I was still in a funk about my mother when Benjy came home from the library. He went up to his room and shut the door. I didn't hear a peep from him about the letters, although I knew he must have seen them. Just like my mother, Benjy left me feeling excluded, not telling me about whatever plans he was making.

I knew it was childish, but I decided I was going to try one of those little passive-aggressive experiments, trying my hardest to hold out and not ask Benjy about college, nor call my mother about anything. I would wait for them to make the effort.

My husband, Roger, came home at 6:30 to find me in the bedroom with the lights off and the covers pulled up to my chin.

"What's going on?" he asked.

"My mother is too busy to talk to me, and our son doesn't want to tell me anything about Pace," I pouted. I started to cry. "I don't want to sound like a whiny five-year-old, but it's really upsetting me. Everybody's leaving me."

He sat down on the bed. "I'm not going anywhere," he said. "We wanted the kids to grow up, remember? All those years of carpools and orthodontia and play rehearsals, you were counting the days until he left the house."

"I know," I said. "And he's probably not going far. I just... oh, I'm tired." I pulled the covers over my head, trying to retreat back into my cave of sorrow.

"I'm sure it's going to be fine. How was class today?" he asked.

"Pretty good." Perking up, I took the covers off and told him how I'd matched up the group of ladies. "They seem to be having a much better time now that they're making friends."

"That's great!" he said. "You need to find a mahj group too."

"You're probably right about that," I said. "I need to find *something*."

"It's April. The days are getting longer," he said. "Let's go to the City this weekend, catch a movie, and walk around Central Park." He was trying very hard to raise my spirits.

"You'd pass up going to Citi Field?" I was surprised. Roger loved baseball more than almost anything, except me, of course, and the Reds were going to be in town for the weekend.

"We could do both..." he said hopefully. "Saturday afternoon in Queens, Saturday evening in Manhattan...?"

I countered his proposal: "How about we see the game on Saturday and do the movie and Central Park on Sunday?"

"Perfect. So what's this about Benjy and Pace?"

CHAPTER 4

Roger's comment—"You need to find a mahj group too"—had touched a nerve with me. It had been years since I played in a regular weekly game. Suddenly I felt that absence.

Back in the day, my group had been very important to me. There were five of us: Ilene, Amy, Stacey, Laurie, and me. We began playing together in our early thirties.

The five of us had each learned to play when we were kids. Our mothers and grandmothers taught us, and the game was as familiar to us as the ABCs. We'd all moved to the same suburban area after getting married, and somehow, between Gymboree, Mommy and Me, and preschool classes at the synagogue, we'd gravitated together. We got together every Tuesday night, taking turns as hostess. It was an established routine for almost eight years.

We had a great time talking and playing, figuring out which teachers to request at the elementary school, finding out about good sales or vacation ideas. We compared bad pediatrician stories and shared tooth fairy sagas. We passed along the names of reliable babysitters. We even shared bad times, like the medical scares involving our kids, our husbands, our parents, or even, sometimes, ourselves. We served as one another's sounding board and support for all sorts of young-mom issues.

There were even a few memorable weekends, when we convinced our husbands and mothers to watch the kids while we went on spa getaways or to nearby mahj tournaments. We found out that Laurie was a compulsive QVC shopper and a real lightweight when it came to alcohol. After one glass of wine, she would laugh hysterically for ten minutes and then fall asleep. We discovered that Amy would eat red velvet anything, was fanatical about doing her yoga stretches, and snored really loudly. Ilene loved to watch PBS cartoons, even if there weren't any children around, and was constantly misplacing things: her keys, her purse, her glasses—and definitely her mah jongg card. Stacey was a very nervous highway driver, never turned down dark chocolate, and needed our help to balance her checkbook. We knew a lot about one another, and we had a tight bond.

Alas, even perfect things must come to an end. The problem was that two among us were sisters. Ilene and Amy were only fifteen months apart and, to be honest, Amy was always copying her big sister. They'd had a double wedding at the synagogue, and Amy had insisted on planning a honeymoon at the same Aruba resort as Ilene. When Ilene bought a Honda Odyssey minivan, Amy had to buy one with the same color and features. When Ilene updated her kitchen, Amy insisted on using the same contractor.

I once described all this to Roger. "If I were Ilene, I would have put my foot down years ago. I understand the wedding—they were doing their parents a favor, combining costs—but going to the same place for their honeymoon? Seriously?"

"Maybe the husbands got along," he said, looking for the silver lining.

"Even if they did," I said, "who wants to double-date on a honeymoon?"

One day Amy went too far even for the ever-patient Ilene. Both sisters had children in the Hey class (fifth grade) at the Hebrew school. Amy's daughter Zoe was two months older than Ilene's son Noah. When the synagogue gave out the official Bar and Bat Mitzvah dates, in order by birthdate, Amy reserved Le Grand Trianon, the catering hall that Ilene had been planning to use. This was apparently the last straw: Ilene said, "There's no way that we can have the exact same party for the kids. No way."

The rabbi offered to let the children share a service, and therefore share their reception, but Ilene was having none of it. She had wanted things a certain way for her son's party. Her husband's extended family was bigger than Amy's husband's and Noah was the first male grandchild on both sides. She had been organizing the event since his bris, the week after his birth. Splitting his big day with his cousin Zoe was not part of her plan. Ilene had already given up center stage at her wedding and total privacy on her honeymoon. Enough was enough.

Amy, on the other hand, felt that Ilene was being selfish. "Zoe is willing to share her service with Noah. She'll be able to help him with chanting the *haftarah*, and all the speeches. It was going to be too hard for him to handle all of it alone. You should be grateful."

Oh, no she didn't. That last comment was beyond the pale, as far as Ilene was concerned. Everyone knew that girls matured faster than boys. Besides, Noah's voice was changing while Zoe was gifted musically. Ilene felt it was a low blow.

Their poor mother. Mrs. Melvin watched her daughters carry on an extended feud and she was caught in the middle.

No one suffered more than she did—except for Stacey, Laurie, and me. We couldn't have a game with just Amy or just Ilene, because that would mean that we favored one over the other. We still attempted to get together as a group of five, but the atmosphere was unbearably tense. Most of the hostility came from Ilene.

An example: someone had exposed three Red Dragons with a Joker. The Joker could be redeemed by whoever got the fourth Red. If Amy happened to pick up the Red and said, "I'd like the Joker," Ilene would make some comment like, "Sure you would. What else do you want?"

It got ugliest when they were seated across from each other. At the end of the passing, or Charleston, the players on the North and South sides of the table had to negotiate a number of tiles for the optional pass. Meanwhile, East and West would reach their own agreement. It wasn't so easy when Amy had to negotiate with Ilene.

Ilene would narrow her eyes and glare at Amy, as if to say, "Go ahead, pick a number. I dare you."

Amy would say, "Whatever you want."

"Because whatever I want, you're just going to say the exact same thing, right?" Ilene would snarl. "I don't even want to go there. I'd rather give you nothing."

"Okay, then," Amy replied. "That's what I wanted, anyway."

There's an implicit rule about privacy, trust, and the sanctity of the mah jongg table: "What's said at the table stays at the table." Unfortunately, it didn't seem to work, in reverse—their family drama had *spread* to the table, and there was nothing that the rest of us could do about it.

At first we tried to remain neutral, but eventually people

started taking sides. Laurie said to me, confidentially: "I don't see why Amy had to pick the Trianon. Ilene had been talking about having the party there for years."

I agreed. "Amy still has almost two years to put something else together."

Stacey, on the other hand, sided with Amy. The two of them had always been best friends, and they had roomed together at the University of Delaware for four years. She said, "There's no reason they can't both have their parties at the same place. They're going to be having different colors, different themes. No one's going to notice."

I allowed that Stacey had a point. "That's true, there will be forty other kids having parties that year. Ilene's not the only one who'll be using it."

The score remained tied: Amy 2, Ilene 2. Mrs. Melvin and I were stuck in the middle. In the end, neither of them could use Le Grand Trianon because the owner was forced to close down—something to do with a food poisoning incident at a wedding reception. Amy threw Zoe's party at the local Marriott, and Ilene had a reception for Noah at a country club. The damage was done, though, and our group fell apart.

———

I'd never had a consistent weekly game since then. Maybe I was afraid that things would just end bitterly, the way my first game had. Maybe I wasn't ready to trust another group on a regular basis. It was kind of like dating: was I willing to give away so much of myself and open up to new people, only to be disappointed?

I occasionally played mah jongg with my mom and a few of her friends. When Harriet Freiman was still around, we would invite a fourth and play for hours. The ladies at Parnassus Pines were funny, and good company. I would hear about the merits of various prescription plans, and the best place to get a colonoscopy or physical therapy. They brought me up to speed on the latest celebrity gossip because some of the ladies were practically addicted to the E! channel. It just wasn't the same as having a regular group, though. I missed my girls.

The college mail kept coming to the house, addressed to Benjy. I was a model of self-restraint as I continued to leave the various envelopes—thin or thick, standard or large—on his bed. Rather than force him into a conversation that he didn't want to have, I was willing to wait him out and listen when he was ready to talk.

Roger, of course, wanted this to be sooner than later. "Does he realize that there's money involved?" he asked me. "Does he just think that, magically, whichever school he picks is going to fit into our budget?"

We were having this conversation on Saturday morning while driving across the George Washington Bridge, heading toward Queens and Citi Field. Roger seemed surprised at my calm, reserved attitude. "Why aren't you needling him?"

"I figure he'll talk to us when he's ready. You know how Benjy is," I added. "Don't you remember middle school when we had to beg him to get out of bed or do his homework? There was a time when I wasn't sure if he'd even *apply* to college. Let's just be a little patient."

Benjy had always been slightly different from his peers, a fish out of water. I thought he just wasn't motivated, but one day I found out that the things he cares about, he cares about deeply.

Halfway through his sophomore year of high school, we took a trip together into New York City. Instead of the usual visit to the Hayden Planetarium, Benjy asked to go to the Cooper Hewitt Museum, which is dedicated to historical and contemporary design. It was his idea—I had no clue he even liked art and design. This kid who I used to worry about—the one who never fit in, who had few friends and stayed locked in his room every weekend—lit up as he walked around the exhibits. He talked with the curators, people my age and older, and had them completely transfixed. He was articulate; he was inquisitive; he was in his element. It was a joy for a mother to watch.

From that moment on, I knew Benjy would be okay. It was a little like the Ugly Duckling—after all those years forcing him to try Cub Scouts and swim team and sleepaway camp, I realized I had been trying to push him into the wrong flock.

In fact, most of the colleges he applied to were design programs in and around New York City. I had a feeling that he might never come back to New Jersey, but I was sure that he'd be happy.

I'd reached a kind of Zen state about Benjy's leaving the nest: I was ready to stand back and let him fly. Of course every mother wants to protect her kids, but I knew he would turn out much stronger if he made his own way. On the other hand, Roger was right—as the ones paying the bills, it would be helpful for us to know exactly how much money was involved.

"Remember, we filled out the FAFSA forms, so each school has a pretty good picture of what we can afford. We'll probably end up paying about the same amount no matter where he goes," I said. "I'll tell you what. If we get to April fifteenth and he still hasn't told us anything, you can put his feet to the fire."

"Me?" Roger asked. He had hoped that I would take charge. "Maybe we could do it together."

"Let's just see how it goes," I said. "We still have ten days or so."

We pulled into the massive parking lot and walked up to the ticket counter. Sadly for the Mets, it wasn't that hard to get tickets on the day of the game. It was still a bit chilly in early April, and we were willing to settle for seats in the upper deck, near the left field foul pole.

Roger wanted to watch batting practice, so I offered to go get some food from Shake Shack. While I was waiting on line, I heard an oddly familiar voice.

"Sam, I told your dad we'd be right back with his order. I don't know if we have time to stand on line for pictures with Mr. Met."

I turned around to see a middle-aged woman who bore a striking resemblance to my old friend Jodi Albert—at least, she looked like Jodi would probably look as a middle-aged woman, like Mrs. Albert looked when we were kids. I must have been staring, because she paused and looked back at me.

"Talia Klein?" she asked.

"Jodi Albert?" I asked in reply.

Jodi's young companion, a tween-age boy in a full, miniaturized Mets ensemble (jacket, t-shirt, baseball pants) looked bored. "Aunt Jodi, come on!"

"Sam, just wait, I want to say hello to someone," she told him. "Talia, wow! I haven't seen you in years!"

"I know," I said. "How are you?"

"Busy. Life. You know," she said, shrugging. "Where are you living?"

"I'm still in the same place, pretty much. If you come back to Jersey sometime, you should call me. It's Welt, now, that's my married name—W-E-L-T."

"Huh! Good to know. Sorry, I have to keep an eye on my nephew. I thought we were getting some burgers, but apparently we're meeting Mr. Met. Enjoy the game!" she said, as he tugged at her impatiently. She disappeared into the crowd, heading toward the Fan Fest region of the stadium.

I got our burgers and fries and headed back to the seats. "You'll never guess who I ran into!" I said as I handed Roger his lunch.

"Who?" he asked gamely.

"Jodi Albert!"

"You're right, I would have never guessed. Who is that?"

I said, "I grew up with her. She and I drifted apart by the time we got to high school, but when I was little we did a lot together. Preschool, Hebrew school. We were even in the same bunk for a few years at sleepaway camp."

He nodded reflexively. I could see he was absorbed in the pregame posting of each team's lineup.

"I just realized the last time I spoke to her," I said. "She paid a shiva call when my dad died. It was awkward."

Roger turned to me. "I'm sorry she brought up memories from such a rough time."

"No, that's okay. I mean, it's over thirty years ago now. I just hadn't given her much thought. So who's pitching?" He showed me the scorecard, and then we both stood up. They were about to begin the National Anthem.

While watching the game, I reflected on my past relationship with Jodi. We'd started out on the same track, doing all those childhood activities. She had gone to a rival high school and then to college in the Midwest, while I went up to study in New England. I sometimes heard about her through Facebook. For instance, I knew that she'd gone to business school and was living a high-powered New York City life.

The childhood memories were still pretty strong. Our dads were both attorneys. Mine had worked at a large Manhattan firm, while hers had stayed local, representing small businesses. Our moms were friendly through the synagogue and women's clubs and I vaguely recalled seeing Mrs. Albert in our living room, playing mah jongg or bridge.

I thought about the last time I spoke with Jodi, during that shiva call at our house. The Albert family—mother, father, Jodi, and her much younger brother, Peter—sat in our living room. Jodi nervously ate chocolate-covered almonds while Mr. and Mrs. Albert talked quietly with my mom. Peter looked bored.

"Do you want to come upstairs?" I asked her. She nodded and we went up to my room.

There was an awkward silence between us. At camp, we had been in different cliques: she was tall, "popular," and much better at sports, while I was fairly uncoordinated, as well as bookish and shy. Although I sometimes saw her at synagogue for the High Holidays or at local youth group parties, we hadn't said anything important to one another for about two years, until that day.

"I'm really sorry about your dad," she said. "Was it a total surprise?"

I nodded. I was hoping she wouldn't ask for all the gory details. There weren't too many: he'd been working late in his office in Manhattan and he collapsed at his desk. The cleaning crew found him at around 10 p.m. and the paramedics rushed over, but he couldn't be revived. Needless to say, we never got a chance to say goodbye. And, yes, forty-four was young. He wasn't thin, by any means, but he seemed healthy enough. He didn't smoke, and he walked a mile each way from the Port Authority bus terminal to his office and back, every day. No one saw it coming.

I said that part aloud. "No one. We were planning to go on a family trip next month. Nobody was expecting this to happen."

She nodded. "I'm really sorry." There wasn't a whole lot more to say. We flipped through an old camp yearbook. She told me stories, gossiped about what was going on with some of the girls from our bunk, people whom I didn't care about. I know she meant to be kind, but I was numb at the time.

That's what I remember most—not feeling anything when she talked, and it's probably why I had avoided her for so many years since. We grew up in adjacent towns, but this huge dividing line arose between us, so the only feeling I associated with her was that numbness.

It's not like we were ever extremely close, but it was funny running into her. I'd given her my married name; maybe I would look up her parents, or she'd find me, and we could spend some time together.

Then I thought about it for a moment: *Jodi is a hotshot New York City success. She'd never bother with a suburban housewife and mah jongg instructor.*

CHAPTER 6

The first Passover seder was a few days later, on April fourteenth, just one day before the deadline Roger and I had set to confront Benjy. We made up an intimate group: Roger, Benjy, me, our daughter Abby and her boyfriend Ethan, my mother, and my uncle, Fred.

It felt a little awkward, seeing my mother. I'd been following through on my plan to let both her and Benjy set the pace of the conversation. I hadn't called Mom, and was waiting for her to contact me. The problem was, she still wasn't calling—not on a daily basis, anyway. I might hear from her twice a week, tops, and the phone calls were always brief: "I'm fine, just checking in." I still couldn't account for the change in our relationship.

Uncle Fred, on the other hand, was just as he'd always been. He was my mother's twin brother and had been a steady presence in our lives ever since my father died. He gave me away at my wedding; he was there for all the bar and bat mitzvahs and family holidays. He was Mom's official escort, and was especially welcome at all those parties because he was such a great dancer.

This arrangement worked well for my mother. She always turned up with Uncle Fred when an occasion called for it. Then again, she was only forty-one when she lost my dad. She'd been pretty and outgoing. Surely, at some point, she'd contemplated getting married again?

I once asked her about it. She explained: "Your father was as much a part of me as my right arm—I couldn't imagine marrying anyone else. Besides, even when I thought about dating again, most of the men my age were looking at women in their twenties and thirties. The only men interested in women my age were already in their sixties, and what did I want with an old man? I go places with my friends, sometimes with couples, but more and more of us are becoming widows." She'd seemed completely comfortable with her situation.

The seder was as full of tradition as ever. We recounted the Passover story and, when it was time for dinner to begin, I asked the kids to come into the kitchen to help me. Abby was now in law school. Never shy, she had always been willing to talk about things that no one else would broach. For instance, she felt no qualms about pushing her little brother.

"Have you made up your mind yet about which college?" she asked.

Benjy looked like he'd just woken up from a long nap. "Huh?" Had it not occurred to him that the rest of us would want to know?

"Mom said you've gotten all sorts of envelopes in the past few weeks," she said, carrying a salad bowl. "What's it gonna be?"

He followed her in with a plate of potato kugel. "I thought I had a couple more weeks to decide," he said. They both sat down at the table.

"Uh—maybe you want to share your thoughts with us?" she prodded. "Come on, Mom and Dad have raised you for eighteen years, they deserve to have a little insight into the process."

If Abby's career goal was to be an advocate on behalf of those who could not speak for themselves, she definitely had chosen the right path. I was stunned at her lack of tact but, on the other hand, appreciated her persistence. "They're the ones who'll be paying for it, for heaven's sake," she added. Roger beamed. He seemed pleased that the law school tuition, at least, was paying for itself.

"Actually," Benjy said, "some of the schools are offering me scholarships."

Roger dropped his fork—quietly, but I noticed. I looked across at him, trying to indicate that he shouldn't overreact. "Sweetheart, that's wonderful!" I said. "We had no idea. Not that you don't deserve one…but maybe, could you tell us a little more about your options?"

Benjy proceeded to share some of the offers he'd received. Some schools had mentioned paid internship possibilities, while others offered tuition assistance or partial merit scholarships. He was carefully weighing the options.

"I want to be in the City, if possible. Some of the better offers came from schools that are more remote, and I don't know whether I want to spend another four years in the suburbs. Not if I don't have to," he added.

Roger pushed back his chair. "Scholarships. Huh." As usual, Benjy had surprised us.

CHAPTER 7

The woman sitting across from me had a few dark flecks of mascara falling onto her cheeks, but otherwise her makeup was flawless. Thick, but flawless. Reading glasses hung from a chain around her neck, and she was very abruptly turning tiles over, crashing them against one another, and using the rack to push them toward the middle of the table.

"Where ya from?" she asked, squinting at my name tag.

"Oh, New Jersey," I replied. "And you?"

"Staten Island. I came with friends," she said. "There are six of us. I'm Vera." She pointed at her name tag.

"Talia," I said, pointing at my own. "Nice to meet you."

We were sitting at one of thirty-six tables, waiting for two other ladies to join us to begin the fourth round of a weekend mah jongg tournament. It was run by an organization based in the New York metropolitan area. There were three days of play, twelve rounds total. I used to come down to their events with the girls from my old group, but it must have been ten years since the last time I'd been there. Vera looked like one of the women I would have played against back then, but of course now we were both older—she looked to be in her early sixties, and I was fifty myself.

"Are you new here?" Vera asked me, as if she'd been reading my mind.

"No. I used to play, but it's been a long time."

"Welcome back. They made you a West. That means

they expect you to know the rules. If I win, you have to sign the score sheet." She laughed. "Big responsibility."

"That's fine," I said. "I'm happy to do it."

The other ladies joined us, a North from Connecticut and a South from Long Island, and Vera rolled the dice to break the wall. "Good luck, ladies," she said.

Since the seder last month, I'd been teaching the new card to ladies in Clubhouses all over northern New Jersey, but as usual I wasn't making any friends. Standing in front of a group didn't offer much of an opportunity for socializing. The relationship was inherently lopsided.

The other problem with teaching was that I hadn't had a chance to actually *play* much mah jongg. Once again, I wished I had a regular group to keep my skills intact. I had hoped to fill in with my mother's group, as needed, but she hadn't invited me in weeks. In fact, she had originally planned to come to this tournament with me. We'd signed up for it back in October. Two weeks before the event, she had backed out, saying only that she needed to cancel. I hadn't expected to come by myself and I wasn't properly prepared, mentally. I was unfocused and distracted by her absence.

The advantage of participating in a tournament was that it gave me a chance to play a lot of mahj over a short period of time, but it wasn't the same as the weekly experience. Needless to say, it lacked the opportunity for camaraderie. At a tournament, you move from table to table every fifty minutes or so, and there isn't much time to get to know your opponents. Then again, fifty minutes with certain individuals can be more than enough for a lifetime.

For instance, Vera turned out to be a pretty ruthless player. She had sized up the North, immediately, as someone who wasn't ready for tournaments. I could see it in the way Vera drummed her impressively lacquered fingernails on the table—she was not even trying to hide her impatience. She sighed as North held up the Charleston, unable to put three tiles together for a first left pass as quickly as the rest of us had. I tried smiling across the table at her to ease the tension, but Vera just exhaled heavily. North flinched.

This was the problem with tournaments. Sometimes the kind people were not very good players, and the good players were not very kind.

Then again, it was so gratifying when I faced someone who was both smart and patient, willing to accept the inadequacies of some of the rookies at the table. I liked to call this type a true "mahj maven," or expert. As we waited, the maven was capable of holding an intelligent conversation while politely encouraging our slower opponent to continue. I loved having mahj mavens at my table, and I made an effort to thank each as we ended our round together.

Overall, I'd had a pretty bad showing so far. I hadn't had much luck at picking Jokers, and without them it was difficult to make most hands. I tried to stay alert to the tiles the other players exposed, hoping for an opportunity to pick up Jokers by exchanging.

Suddenly, in the fifth round, I picked all the right tiles. I was able to exchange for Jokers almost as soon as they were exposed. Perhaps someone hadn't mixed the tiles well—that was a good explanation for why I kept redeeming other people's missing tiles—but whatever the reason, I was the bene-ficiary. I won three out of the four hands in the round, and the last was a real long-shot: a Quint hand. I made it after exchanging for three Jokers.

The South player for that round was a woman named Lisa. She had glasses and dark, curly hair, and looked to be about my age. She said, "Wow, you're really on fire! How have you been doing, this tournament?"

"Poorly," I confessed. "I only made mahj twice before this round. I had 80 points after four rounds."

"I've seen worse," she said. "You never know when you're going to hit a hot streak."

"I guess," I sighed. "I wish it had happened earlier. I feel like I'm too far out of it to win."

"One more round and then we break for lunch," Lisa said. "Do you want to sit together? I'll save you a seat." Thrilled at being asked and smiling broadly, I gladly accepted.

Of course, my sixth round was as dismal as the first four had been. When I found Lisa in the dining room, I showed her my personal scorecard. "I think I should have just stayed at our table for the rest of the day," I said.

She laughed. "I know how you feel. I couldn't figure out a good hand. There are times when I look at the tiles and I completely blank out. I can't remember normal sequences. It gets overwhelming, playing for so many hours like this."

"It's a lot," I agreed, "but it's my only option. It's like a mahj binge. I don't have a regular weekly game, so I wanted to come to a tournament to play as much as I could."

"Where are you from?" she asked.

I told her that I lived in New Jersey and that I was a mah jongg instructor.

"So am I," she said. "About an hour west of Philadelphia."

"Funny," I said. "Where do you teach?"

"At a community center and at a senior residence place—fifty-five and up."

I started laughing. "I think we're living the same life. Do you have a regular group?"

"No," she admitted. "I used to, but we broke up, for a really sad reason."

"Sounds familiar. What happened to yours?"

She looked around cautiously. "Eh, nobody around here would know them." She leaned in conspiratorially. "One of the girls was having an affair and used to talk about it while we played. Even when we were playing in her living room while her husband was upstairs. I wasn't going to tell him…"

"Sanctity of the table," I said. "I get it."

She continued, "I felt extremely uncomfortable knowing he was right there. I had to quit the group."

I nodded. "Mine broke up because two of the players had an ongoing feud. They were sisters." I told Lisa about the double-date honeymoon and the ridiculous bar and bat mitzvah stress, and she laughed.

"All sorts of crazy stuff happens," she said. "Live long enough and you'll hear every kind of story."

"So you come to tournaments to play, since you can't otherwise?" I asked.

"Pretty much," she admitted. "It's hard to find people our age who take it seriously."

"If there are two of us, I'm sure there are more," I said.

"Do you teach your friends?"

"Most of them are still tied up in their kids. My youngest is about to graduate high school."

"Same," I laughed.

"It's too far to travel for a weekly game, but maybe we'll meet up at another tournament," she told me. I took down her email address and gave her mine.

After lunch, we continued with the Saturday afternoon rounds. I did as poorly as I had for most of the morning. My heart just wasn't in it. I kept dwelling on the past. I recognized that my mother had her own life and it made me sad to think of how my old mahj friends had all gone their own ways. The afternoon games ended, and I watched as groups of four and five laughed together. I half-expected to see Stacey or Laurie come walking down the steps from the lobby, but of course that wasn't going to happen.

When I got back to my hotel room, I called Roger. "I'm not cut out for these things anymore," I told him. "I shouldn't have come by myself."

"What happened?" he asked patiently.

"I'm not winning, which is okay, but I just feel weird. I haven't come back to this place since the old days, and being here makes me miss the people who aren't around. I guess I was counting on having my mom come with me this time. Did she call at all this weekend?"

"Not a peep," he said. "Benjy and I were just about to sit down to some pasta. I made a salad."

"Good for you!" I said.

"Do you want to come home?" he asked me.

"I can't," I explained. "The room's already paid for and I have to be here to play in the morning. It's not right to abandon a tournament mid-event. People expect you to stay for the whole thing."

"True, it wouldn't be fair," he said. "Still...you don't sound good."

"Oh, I'll be all right," I said. "I'll see you tomorrow afternoon, sometime after two."

I hung up. I thought of Jodi Albert and wondered what she was doing. I imagined her living some exciting, jam-packed New York City life—Broadway shows, nightclubs, four-star restaurants. Even if I had her number, I was sure she wouldn't have time to chat with me.

I remembered that I had the email address for Lisa, my fellow tournament-goer. "I know this is insane, we're in the same hotel," I typed, "but I don't know your last name, or what room you're in. Want to come out for dinner?"

About four minutes later, she emailed back. "Sure!"

We found an Outback Steakhouse five miles down the road and had a pleasant dinner, sharing stories and comparing our similar lives. We each had two kids and had been married more than twenty years.

She took another sip of her Shiraz. "You're going to be my tournament pal!" she enthused. "We'll have to figure out where to go next year. Arizona, maybe, or Las Vegas."

"That seems pretty far afield. Let's start with Atlantic City," I suggested. She agreed.

"Must be that glass of wine I had," she said. "I should get

back to the room before I conk out." I smiled to myself, thinking of how Laurie had been almost the exact same way.

———

I drove us back to the hotel. When I came into the lobby, there was Roger standing with a little rolling suitcase. I flung my arms around him.

"Who's your boyfriend?" Lisa asked.

"Oh, this is Roger. Roger Welt, Lisa…"

"Baker," she said. "Nice to meet you."

I explained that Lisa was from Philadelphia and that we'd just gone out to dinner. Lisa excused herself and I hugged Roger again. "What are you doing here?"

"I wolfed down the pasta and jumped in the car," he said. "Benjy is fine on his own. You sounded so forlorn, I just figured that I'd better come down here." He gestured at the suitcase. "Can I come up to the room?"

"That's a great idea," I said. "My weekend has just improved dramatically."

CHAPTER 8

The phone rang. For once, the caller ID said "Frances Klein." I eagerly picked up the phone.

"Hi, Mom, what's up?"

"Nothing much. I was wondering if you could stop by on Tuesday after class?" I couldn't remember the last time she'd initiated a call. Over the past two weeks, ever since that tournament, I'd only called her twice. She had never even asked about it.

I was glad that she wanted to see me. "Yeah, I think I can be there at about 2. Should I bring anything?" I asked.

"No, that's fine. Just come by."

"And you're feeling okay?" I was trying to get any information from her that I could, but to no avail.

"Sure. Everything's great. Just saw the doctor, he says that my blood pressure's where he wants it to be. I'm doing fine. Gotta go!"

"Okay, see you Tuesday."

I hung up, thoroughly confused. What was this bizarre change that had come over my mother?

Even if *our* relationship had deteriorated, I knew that she was still getting together with Benjy. Ever since he got his driver's license, two years ago, we'd let him go wherever he wanted after school, on the condition that he texted us with updates. I'm sure there are other teenagers who might text, "Working at the library," or "Having dinner with grandma," and then skip out to the mall or to a diner with friends—but Benjy wasn't that kind of kid. If he was going to the mall, he'd say so: "Checking out the window displays, home by 8:30."

He always came home when he said he would and when he said he was with his grandmother, I had no reason to doubt him. At least once a week, and often more, he'd meet up with her. Though neither would tell me anything about it, I was glad that they still spent quality time together.

———

Tuesday was the last session of "Level Two"—Becky and her new friends had asked me to extend the class because they wanted to learn more strategy. Her little foursome was getting along beautifully. Many of the other ladies also had warmed up to one another, and we were looking forward to having a kind of "graduation party." I was to bring popcorn and they would each bring homemade treats.

My students came in, enthusiastically greeting one another. *What a difference from those first two sessions*, I thought.

"Are you coming to Movie Night tonight?" asked Cheryl. "I think it's *Dr. Strangelove.*"

"Of course," said Becky. "Wouldn't miss it. Charlie says he'll come too, if Henry will be there."

I thought that it was adorable. Their husbands were even becoming friends, and they were going on double dates. I couldn't be more pleased.

"Let's go to the diner first," said Cheryl. "Anyone else want to come with us?"

They set up at three separate tables and I wandered among them, observing how each group was playing. At the far table, I overheard two of the students talking about last week's Casino Night at the Clubhouse.

"Did you see Marty going around with a new girlfriend, what's her name, Sherry? For a while there, I thought he was serious with Fran, they'd been together for months," said the first, Ronnie.

My ears perked up at the name. Ronnie continued, throwing out a tile: "Three—what is this? Three Crak."

"Oh, you can't trust Marty Wolf. He's been divorced three times already. Fran wasn't expecting anything long term with him," said the player sitting next to her, Millie. "West."

Grace, another woman at their table, said, "Seven Bam. Are we playing here, or what? Please stop the gossip and focus on the game."

Fran was a common name in Parnassus Pines, so I didn't think twice about their conversation.

"That Sherry, she must have been some looker," said Marlene, the fourth player. "Gorgeous eyes. Two Bam."

"Oh, please," said Grace. "Can we just finish the game?"

"I don't even remember who threw last," said Ronnie.

"I did," said Marlene. "Two Bam."

"Call it," said Millie. "Mah jongg." She already had four One Bams exposed, but put up three more Two Bams, showing a sequence of four Flowers, four One Bams, four Two Bams, and two Green Dragons.

Grace sighed in disgust. "Uch. I didn't think you had the dragons too. Fine. Tell us all about what happened."

The drama in Parnassus Pines was usually pretty benign. A person inadvertently insulted someone else by not inviting them to go someplace or it got around that they received a present that was regifted, or another similar *faux pas*. These things could easily fester and grow into something huge unless the two parties were seen in public together almost immediately. Sometimes they were almost forced to have a feud, to keep the gossips satisfied. People loved to add fuel to the fire: "Barbara, dear, I can't believe Ellen went and gave you the coasters that Audrey gave her a month ago! She even reused the wrapping paper!"

I was expecting more of the same trivial nonsense. Ronnie emptied her rack onto the middle of the table. The others started mushing the tiles around as they listened to her story.

"I heard that Marty started driving Sherry around on some little errands. You know what I mean. Nothing big, just taking her to the eye doctor, helping her carry big boxes to the Pack 'n' Ship place." Ronnie looked meaningfully at the others. "But then he stood Fran up."

Grace stared her down. "How would you know?"

"Oh, I know these things. I ran into Fran one afternoon at Trader Joe's. She had a lot in her shopping cart, told me Marty was coming over that night for dinner...three hours later, she invited me to come by. She said she had too many leftovers because he never came."

Marlene shook her head. "I liked them together. Fran is a smart cookie. She was really good for him."

"She was *too* good for him," said Millie. "She should have dumped him right away."

"Yeah, and Marty has a wandering eye. It was probably all because of Sherry," said Ronnie.

"I wouldn't trust her around *my* husband, that's for sure," said Marlene.

I couldn't help listening, but I wanted to get the ladies to refocus on the mah jongg.

"Millie, that was a great hand!" I said. "Who threw that Two Bam?"

"I did," said Marlene. "I thought she didn't have enough Green Dragons."

"It's important to look at all the discards," I explained. "Keep an eye on what's been thrown." I looked at the clock. "It's about time to go. Let's gather up the tiles and have some of those great snacks!"

I sat off to one side, distractedly nibbling on one of Ronnie's homemade dream bars, while the ladies raved about their friends' creations. During that entire conversation, I'd never heard anyone mention a last name. There were plenty of Frans and plenty of smart cookies in the neighborhood. My mother had never been interested in dating, or so she said, but she'd never been so absent like this before. Maybe she had been dating? It would explain a lot.

I checked the time on my cell phone repeatedly. I was looking forward to stopping by at two o'clock and having a little chat with Fran.

I psyched myself up all the way over to my mother's house. I could play detective and ask her if she knew anyone named Marty. Or maybe I should play dumb and just ask about what she'd been up to all this time? I decided I should see how she was feeling. After all, these ladies said that Marty had moved on to someone else. Maybe she had called me because she was heartbroken.

I was on the next block, looking for an open space in the Visitor Lot, when I saw Jodi Albert getting out of a little silver Lexus. I pulled up beside her, opened my window, and said, "Hey, stranger! Fancy meeting you here!"

Jodi did a double-take. "Talia, hey. Does your mother live in Parnassus Pines?"

"Yep, about nine years already. Oh, geez, I'm so sorry. Wait a second." I finished parking next to her and got out of the car.

"Oh, Jodi, I feel terrible. I totally forgot about your dad." He'd passed away around Thanksgiving last year. "I didn't know about it until after New Year's, I read it in the synagogue bulletin. I should have written you a note." I felt even more awkward about not having mentioned it the first time I ran into her, at Citi Field. "I'm so sorry for your loss."

"Thank you. We're doing all right. Dad had emphysema for the last six years and, honestly, toward the end he was just glad to let go. It was pretty awful."

I listened, nodding quietly. "It's good that your mom still has you and Peter."

"Yeah, she 'sold' the house to him and moved in here in January. He and his wife wanted their kids to be in a better school district. Ma's right over there, 17 Delphi Drive."

"Does she like it here?" I asked.

"Sure. Ma's got everything she needs. Still goes to synagogue, shops at the same stores, sees the same people. I think she's finding things to do at the Clubhouse. Where is your mother's place?"

"It's just around the corner, 23 Corinth Court. I'm on my way over to see her," I said. "And I heard you were living in the City?"

"Yes, but…" She looked down for a moment. "I'm kind of in transition. Listen, I have to get over to her place, but we should catch up sometime." She handed me her business card: *Profonex*. "Don't use the office number, but you can text me or call me on my cell."

"Okay, great!" I said. "I'll be in touch."

———

Bumping into Jodi had changed my frame of mind. Just talking with her about losing her dad had given me some perspective. I still wanted to know what my mother had been up to for the past few months, but I decided to take a calm, reserved approach. If she was the Fran they were gossiping about and some guy named Marty had dumped her, she might actually be in a fragile state. There was no point in piling on or making it harder for her.

I rang the doorbell and Mom opened the door quickly.

"Talia, honey," she said, and gave me a big hug. "I've got the greatest news!"

This did not seem like a despondent, jilted woman.

"What? What's going on?"

"I have heard nothing but raves about your classes at the Clubhouse and now the Board wants to have you run a mah jongg tournament!" she said.

"A—wait, what about Lois Benson?" I asked.

My mother waved away the very mention of her name. "Please. She's old news. They specifically requested you. I think it's fantastic! Come in, come sit down."

We walked past the foyer into the living space. It's hard to call it a room, it's more like an alcove—the foyer had a powder room and closet on one side and the alcove with the couch, table, and television on the other side, and if you walked forward a bit there was a dinette set, but the space was too small to be an actual dining room.

This was what I'd rushed past, two months before. I'd gone by the sitting area, kitchen, and laundry machines on my way down the hall to the master bedroom and bath, searching for my mother. It felt like a lot longer than two months that she'd been avoiding me—and yet here she was, standing in her usual purple velour tracksuit, talking like her old self.

We sat down at the table and she pulled out a yellow legal pad. "We've got to get organized!" she said.

"Wait, 'we'?"

"Sure, I'm going to help you run this thing. You're the mahj expert, you'll enforce the rules. I'll do the recruitment and the menu. There's a lot of behind-the-scenes work that goes into making these things happen."

"Oh, I know," I said. "I mean, I've been in a lot of tournaments...there was one just a few weeks ago, in fact."

She brushed off the comment. "They're thinking of mid-November," she said, "before the snowbirds go down to Florida. That gives us plenty of time, almost six months. I know we can do a great job, and we'll get to work together! Oh, I'm so excited!"

Clearly, Fran Klein had moved on to new adventures. She wasn't apologizing for having been so distant, or for standing me up at the tournament. It was my decision whether I wanted to forgive her, so we could move forward on this project.

I've never been one for confrontations. That's much more Abby's style. However, I needed recognition from her, an admission that something had changed, if only to check my own sanity.

"Mom, is there something you want to tell me? I mean, you've been absent and distracted."

She looked up from her yellow pad. "Yes, I would say that I'm no longer distracted. How's that?"

"That's it? Isn't there anything else you want to say?"

She shook her head. "If I feel like talking about it, I'll let you know. Let's leave it at that."

As I was leaving my mother's apartment, I mentioned that I had run into Jodi. I asked if she knew that Mrs. Albert had moved in around the corner.

"Yes," she said, "and she gave her house to her son. Do you remember Peter?"

I nodded. "I was surprised to see Jodi in New Jersey in the middle of the afternoon. I thought she worked in the City."

"Hmm." My mother was noncommittal. "Maybe you should talk to her."

My mother generally had good ideas—after all, she'd steered me toward the teaching job—so I decided to follow up on the suggestion. That evening I left a voice mail on Jodi's cell phone. "Hey, it's Talia Welt. Talia *Klein* Welt. Nice to see you today. Twice in two months, after thirty-five years— it must be a sign. I'm sure you're swamped, but maybe we can get together the next time you're in New Jersey."

Jodi called me back at around 9:15 the next morning and said, "Next week looks good. How's lunch on Tuesday?"

My regular Tuesday class had just ended, so my days were wide open. "That sounds great," I said.

We agreed to meet at Amici, an Italian restaurant about ten miles away from beautiful Parnassus Pines and, therefore, outside either of our mothers' normal travel circles. I was trying to figure out why Jodi would want to spend so much time on this side of the Hudson River, so I looked her up on Facebook.

Facebook was no help—her last post, "Great fireworks," was dated July 4, 2009. She had no pictures or "likes" on her page. She was truly keeping a low profile. I decided to Google her.

Jackpot! Google had a lot of information about a company she'd founded twenty years ago, called Profonex—the one that was listed on her business card. I read about how she was the driving force behind creating user-friendly voice recognition software in the early days of the telecommunications boom. Her company had been quite successful. I found a photo in *Forbes* magazine: Jodi in a business suit, standing with her arms crossed in front of a big desk, with a huge picture window behind her. "Savvy and Single." There were other pictures in *Enterprising Women* and *American Business Monthly*, with similar captions: "A Woman with a Clear Message," "Challenge Accepted."

Then there were *Business Week* photos of her with Profonex Marketing Director Gary Blenhart, from about ten years ago. Pictures of *both* of them, back-to-back, with their arms crossed: "Dynamic Duo." Glamour shots taken of them at black-tie charity events: "Telling a New Story in Telecom." The *Wall Street Journal* ran a short piece when she handed the CEO reins to Gary four years ago, and had a few more articles as the company declined in value over the next three years. I wondered if there was a connection.

The trail, and the dramatic success story, ended when I tried to access the Profonex website. I typed in *www.profonex.com* and got the error message: "Server not found."

———

Jodi was already seated and reading the menu when I got to the Italian place. I felt a little guilty as I slid into the booth across from her. "Listen, I Googled you," I blurted out. "Well, Profonex, anyway."

"So what did you find?" she asked. "I can fill you in on anything you might have missed." She put the menu down. "Did you see 'Savvy and Single'? My mother still has it up on her refrigerator."

"Yeah, saw that one...full color, very nice. Your hair looked great."

She laughed. "I know, right? Remember back at camp, I used to win all the frizz contests?"

I vividly remembered a day when she'd looked like a mad scientist. She'd even received a nickname.

"Oh, sure. Jodi Albert Einstein," I said, laughing. "Man, if only I'd had a camera then. Instant blackmail."

"Well, I'm glad you didn't," she said, chuckling. "They hired the best hairdressers in Manhattan, Madison Avenue's finest, just for that photo session. Two hours later, it was puffy again. Still is." She smiled. "Anyway, you Googled me. You got to see the rise and fall of a Telecom Titan."

"Hence the business number no longer working?" I asked.

She nodded. "Profonex no longer exists. Gary ran it into the ground."

"Sounds thorough. So I guess you're not telling that story together any more?"

"NNN-nope." She looked at the menu, avoiding my eyes. "Middle age is a turnoff, apparently. At least on me."

I was sorry to have upset her. The wound seemed fresh. I tried to build up her confidence.

"He doesn't sound like the brightest bulb," I said. "I mean, you were the woman with the clear message, and he was the one who killed the company."

She sighed. "You've pretty much got the picture. Can we talk about something else? *Anything* else?"

"Absolutely," I said quickly. "I mean, I just wanted you to know that I knew, so that we could get past all that. So how was prom? Who'd you go with?"

She burst out laughing. "Seriously? That was, what, almost thirty-five years ago?"

"And what did you wear?"

"Good thing you couldn't find *that* on Google. I went with Doug Epstein and I wore a long, pink, hideous thing. Have we really not spoken since high school?"

"Not since you paid that shiva call for my dad," I said.

"Oh, I'm so sorry," she said. "I can't believe we never talked at all after that. That seems wrong."

"That's how life gets," I said. "You went west, I went north. You started a business, I got married and raised kids. Now *your* dad's gone too, and our mothers live around the corner from one another. Our paths crossed again."

She held up her water glass. "To reuniting and the blessing of finding an old friend."

I picked mine up and clinked it against hers. "Amen to that."

"I had lunch with Jodi today," I told Roger. "It's so nice to spend time with someone my age, for once."

We were in the bedroom, and he was listening to me with one ear while watching ESPN. "Hmm."

"I've been so upset, the way Benjy and Mom were avoiding me, but here was a person who wanted to talk to me! And it wasn't like when I teach class. We had an actual conversation."

He hmm'd again.

"It seems like we've really hit it off, all these years later. In fact, we're planning to have a double date with George Clooney and Brad Pitt," I said.

"That's great!" he said. "Wait, what?"

I laughed and said, "Go back to the television. I just wanted to tell you that we had fun."

"Yes, I understood that part," he said. "Sorry, I wasn't listening."

———

I thought again about lunch with Jodi. Once I made that initial Google confession, we were able to get past our huge difference in career paths. I was embarrassed to say that I was a mah jongg instructor, but she had no problem with my job: "I think it's great. You're connecting with people and helping them. I'm not even working right now, so who am I to judge?"

I appreciated her support. "So now you have extra time to come out to New Jersey and see your mother?"

"Yes, we still have a lot of loose ends to wrap up with Dad's finances. She filed an extension on her 2013 taxes, because she just wasn't ready with the death certificates and estate documentation, but I'm trying to get all that settled," she said.

"There's always some kind of paperwork," I sighed. "We had to put together this whole pile of information for Benjy to qualify for financial aid, but now it seems like he's getting a scholarship."

"That's great!" she said. "What is he studying?"

"I don't know. Design something. I don't understand it, but he's excited and that's what matters, right?"

She laughed. "That's what I hear. I parent vicariously, with Peter's kids."

"Sam? The little boy at the Mets game?" I asked.

"Yes, Peter and his wife, Nancy, also have a daughter named Lara. She's two years younger. I think it's good that they'll raise the kids in our old house. There's a little closure to it, you know?" Jodi smiled at the thought.

"Was your mother upset about giving up her house?" I asked.

"Ma? No, it was her idea. She knew it was a better neighborhood and I think she would have gone crazy staying in the house with them. Peter's ophthalmology practice is about six miles from here. He sold his old house, bought the place in Parnassus Pines for Ma, and…well, with some creative accounting, everybody will be just fine. She didn't need all that space and now she'll be with lots of other people her own age. She might even make new friends."

I remembered the previous week, when I'd wanted to come in, guns blazing, to ask my mother about Marty.

"Listen, speaking of new friends, let me pick your brain on this. Do you and your mother talk often?" I asked.

"Back when Dad was sick we were always on the phone. Now she calls every couple of days. Sometimes I answer the phone, sometimes I'm out. I don't usually return her call because she'll catch me the next day or two. Why?" she asked.

"My mom and I used to speak every single day. She'd call me and we'd get together at least once a week. Plus she would see Benjy. I know you're not right on top of your mom, the way we are, but let's just say...she was a constant presence. I never wondered what she was up to because I knew."

Jodi shrugged. "Okay. So did something change?"

"Yes!" I said. "Really weird. She suddenly stopped calling, and I had to chase her down. She'd be brief on the phone; she'd go a week without speaking to me. She cancelled some of the dinner plans we'd made, and there was a trip we were going to take." I was momentarily embarrassed to explain. "It was a mah jongg tournament, but I was counting on going with her. Then, two weeks before, she just said she wasn't coming."

"Hmm. Interesting," said Jodi. "And you thought...?"

"I didn't know what to think, frankly," I said. "It's never happened before, and here I was, in the throes of losing Benjy to college, so I was a little distressed."

"And...?" she prompted.

"And then suddenly, out of the blue, she called and said, 'Come on over on Tuesday.' That was last week, when I ran into you in the parking lot."

Jodi nodded, waiting for me to continue.

"I told you that I teach mah jongg at the Pines Clubhouse,

right?" I asked. She nodded again. "That same Tuesday, I overheard some of my students gossiping about a guy who had dumped one of the neighborhood ladies for another. The woman he left was named Fran..."

"Interesting. I guess they didn't know you were her daughter?"

"It could have been another Fran," I argued. "Could have been."

"I don't know, it certainly makes sense to me. And you wouldn't have told me if you didn't suspect it yourself," she said. "It stands to reason: she's suddenly too busy to see you, she's got other things to do...and now that he's dumped her, she's available again."

"But my mom has never dated. All the years since my dad died, she just...I mean, when she was younger, it might have made sense to remarry, but she never wanted to...I don't get it."

"Listen, maybe she just wanted some company. It was a cold winter!" Jodi reasoned.

"Ew! I don't even want to think about it. This was some old guy named Marty. Ew. Stop." I covered my ears, like a six-year-old.

"Please tell me the new lady isn't named Carol. That's the last thing I need, Ma running around with the neighborhood playboy."

"No, they said her name was Sherry. Anyway, so you think my hunch is right?" I asked. "She was dating this guy and he just dumped her?"

"Sounds logical to me," she said. "I think you cracked the case."

We both laughed. "Some great mystery," I said. "The Missing Mom."

We split the bill and headed for the parking lot. "This was nice. We should definitely do it again soon," I told her.

She agreed. "Next time, come into the City. My evenings are pretty busy, so let's stick with lunch."

"I don't want to interfere with your job search," I said.

"Pssh." She waved her hand at me. "I invested well. I don't need to work for anyone else, so I'm just taking it easy. Let's say lunch at one, next Tuesday. We'll go to this Vietnamese place, you'll love it."

"Lunch is perfect, I like to be home for dinner with Benjy and Roger," I said. "I'll see you then!"

Summer

CHAPTER 12

I teach mah jongg in all sorts of communities and have met many people. The ladies get so comfortable and caught up in what they're doing that they forget I'm there, so I have overheard quite a few stories as I've hopped from clubhouse to clubhouse. One thing I've learned is that some people never develop beyond their childhood selves. I saw it myself with the mah jongg crowd at Chestnut Arbor.

Chestnut Arbor is a fifty-and-up development about fifteen minutes south of my town, and it's decidedly upscale. It's exclusive—only 200 units. They have an indoor swimming pool, racquet ball courts, and two tennis courts that are enclosed during the winter. Many of the homes are adjacent to a private golf course. It was built in the 1990s, about ten years before Parnassus Pines.

Most of the condos come with their own two-and-a-half garage: two cars and a separate bay for a golf cart. The development had been designed to attract a more active crowd and people who move there choose it because of the sporting opportunities. Those first buyers have since gone through hip replacements or bursitis, have become more sedentary, and are forced to spend the majority of their time indoors. The turnover is fairly high as the wounded warriors depart and make way for new(er) blood.

The Chestnut Arbor Neighborhood Association had hired me to run a workshop in early July—"How to Switch Your Hand"—and I was invited to come an hour early to join the mah jongg group for lunch. There were fifteen ladies in the room, scattered in groups at the various tables. I sat unobtrusively off to the side, enjoying a chef salad and iced tea, but was waved over by a tall redhead wearing a tremendous amount of makeup. She looked to be in her early seventies yet was still trying to channel Tina Louise, right down to the beauty spot.

"Call me Ginger," she said, and invited me to sit with her and three other ladies at a round table.

Ginger introduced me to Sally, Beverly, and Winnie, and wanted to get me up to speed on their discussion.

"We just came back from a seven-night Bermuda cruise out of Bayonne, on one of the big ships. It was just a girls' trip: Beverly was there, and Sally was my roommate. I'm just explaining to Winnie what she missed." She turned to Winnie. "Next time, you definitely have to come—I think the lineup's going to change, for sure.

"There were eight of us altogether. The other five were Linda Atherton, Linda *Barker*, Betty Haas—you remember Betty, she's the one who used to run a bridal shop. And there were Janet Lang and Maureen Bryce.

"Anyway. We booked four cabins, all together on the same deck, and I had arranged for us to have a table of eight in the dining room…but on the second night, Janet was nowhere to be found!"

The other ladies at the table rolled their eyes a bit, uninterested in adding to the commentary, but Winnie listened eagerly. It was obvious to me that Ginger was used to commanding attention.

"So. Maureen came to breakfast alone the next morning, and didn't say a word about Janet. Didn't say she was sleeping in, didn't say whether she ever came back, never spoke about her at all. Lunchtime came and went. The ship was approaching Bermuda and would be docking the following morning, so I started getting worried. I asked Maureen if she'd mind if I came back with her to their cabin for a moment."

She looked at the others, explaining herself. "You see, I was looking for a clue—something out of the ordinary—but all of Janet's clothes were still there. She'd left her extra shoes but taken her sun hat. Her book bag was also missing. It was a big ship. Maureen thought that maybe Janet was on the resort deck, reading a book."

Ginger took a breath and then continued. There was no stopping her when she was on a roll like this. "The ship had a card room and some of the other girls were playing mah jongg there for a few hours"—at this, Sally and Beverly nodded at me—"but I just had to find Janet. I must have wandered all over the decks for an hour or more. I peeked into the public rooms and lounges. I thought she might be somewhere nursing a Long Island iced tea, or sitting in the library, reading about Bermuda. But when she never turned up—my goodness, what if she'd fallen overboard?!"

"Did she?" asked Winnie, who was hanging on Ginger's every word. The other two ladies just looked away, shaking their heads. Sally actually sighed, having heard the story several times already.

"They have these sensors and cameras," Sally said to me. "Someone is always keeping an eye on the decks and watching to make sure that people don't fall off the boat." She gave me a feeble smile. "They explained that to us when we first came on the ship."

"Well, no, no, she hadn't fallen overboard," Ginger admitted. "Let me finish. I finally gave up looking and returned to the card room to play some mahj. You remember, Beverly, how distracted I was? I passed two Flowers and a Dragon in the Charleston, and I never pass Flowers. I ended up throwing a winning mahj tile twice. I was just too worried about poor Janet.

"We went back to our rooms to change for dinner and I followed Maureen and watched as she opened her cabin door. All of Janet's things were gone! I was so surprised!"

"Maureen said, 'I suppose she moved to another cabin. Looks like she took everything.'

"I asked if we should be worried, and whether she would show up at dinner, and Maureen said she had no idea. We went down to dinner together—Sally, Maureen, and I—and met the two Lindas on the stairs.

"Linda Barker said, 'It's strange. I think I saw Janet at lunchtime at the buffet. This ship is so big, it could have been someone who just looks like her.'"

We were past the time I should have begun the class, but there was no stopping Ginger from telling her tale. "When we docked in Bermuda the next morning, Maureen, Betty, and I went into Hamilton to go shopping. We were in this cute sweater shop, and I overheard Janet's voice. She was talking to a saleswoman about a shade of blue, and how well it would go with her granddaughter's complexion and hair color.

"I spotted her again, on the ship at dinner. She was across the dining room, sitting at a table of men and women. Betty said, 'I guess that's that. She's found another group. Looks like she's happy.'"

Ginger was still indignant at the very thought of it. She addressed Winnie directly. "Can you imagine? We came as a group and she deserted us! We're not good enough for her, apparently. I guess she'll be moving out of the development soon."

"What are you talking about?" Beverly asked. "She's not moving. She's perfectly fine. I think she'll be here this afternoon."

Ginger was aghast. "I—I don't know what to say to her. Sally, are you speaking to her?"

"Of course," said Sally.

Ginger looked confused. The betrayal, the mutiny was just too much for her. "Janet never said *why* she left the room, *why* she stopped sitting with us."

"No, but I imagine she wanted to meet some new people. I don't see why that's such a big deal," said Sally.

"It's inexcusable," said Ginger. "It was disrespectful of her to just disappear and not tell anyone where she'd gone." Winnie nodded, a solemn expression on her face.

"Did Maureen *say* she never told her where she'd gone?" asked Beverly.

"Well...no..." admitted Ginger.

Sally shrugged. "Maybe she and Maureen didn't want to share the room after all. Maybe Janet met some people she really liked. It's not that big a deal."

"All the same," said Ginger, "you can bet I won't be inviting her on our next outing!"

It was all oddly familiar. I thought of when my daughter Abby was in middle school. One afternoon she came home very upset. "Sara wasn't at our table at lunch," she said, "and

I don't think Katie's going to let her come back." Apparently one was supposed to commit to Queen Bee Katie's group forever, and the punishment for straying was banishment... in sixth grade, anyway.

Here in the Chestnut Arbor Clubhouse, Ginger seemed flustered. I wondered if she would repeat her performance from the ship, when she was not able to focus on mah jongg because she was so concerned about Janet. I was trying to picture Janet, this rebel who broke cultural norms by choosing to meet new people on vacation.

I was about to begin my lecture when three more women walked in. One was a Linda, and the other two were the infamous Janet and her neighbor, Annette. I tried to spot anything unique about Janet. Like many of the other ladies, she was in a fancy t-shirt—something from Alfred Dunner or maybe Talbots. Nothing outrageous—no tie-dyed Deadhead shirt or free-spirit, hippie kind of blouse. Nothing particularly trendy. She was carrying a simple leather purse, as well, and wearing the same kind of eyeglass frames as everyone else. No billowing scarves or complicated jewelry—strictly standard-issue accessories.

I welcomed all the ladies and introduced myself. I began the lecture, talking about what kinds of situations we might find ourselves in where we would need to switch our hands. "Obviously, it's best to figure out the new hand early enough in the game so that you still have a chance of winning," I explained. We talked about pairs being unavailable and about new opportunities coming up, like suddenly picking two Jokers or a third Flower. There were all sorts of reasons why you might need to switch your hand.

Some of the ladies talked about how confusing it was to switch. Linda said, "I thought we were supposed to keep trying for a hand and if we couldn't make it, then we should start playing defensively." Others nodded in agreement.

Annette said, "I usually only go for a hand if I already have the pair at the start of the game. That, or I go for a hand where I can use Jokers."

I asked her how often she won. "Usually once an afternoon...sometimes I don't win at all."

"Do tiles ever come in that might point to a better hand?" I asked her.

"Hmm. I don't know, I never really thought about it," she admitted.

I divided the group into tables of four players each to begin a game and hopefully illustrate my points. I unintentionally put Ginger at the same table as Janet, along with Annette and Sally, and the redhead was visibly uncomfortable about it. There was absolutely no chitchat about the cruise.

I walked among the tables, looking for an interesting opportunity, a "teachable moment." I saw one when Annette picked up a third Joker.

"Maybe you can find a Quint hand," I said. "It's early enough in the game. Let's see what your options are."

She switched around her tiles and I helped her identify a combination she hadn't originally considered. She ended up winning the game. When it was over, I showed the others what she'd done.

"Sometimes things come along that you weren't expecting, and you modify your game plan," I said. "Annette picked Jokers and they presented her with new possibilities."

Janet nodded. "I can see that happening. You have to be open to new information, and know when it's time to change course."

Ginger? Not so much.

CHAPTER 13

Jodi and I were sitting on my back patio under a big umbrella, sipping lemonade.

"Did I tell you that Sam is going to Camp Adelaide this summer?" she asked.

"You're kidding," I said. "Peter let him go there?"

"What? He's only ten years old," she said. "What kind of trouble could he possibly get into?"

We both laughed. "I described the place to Roger and he said there was no way that we would ever send Abby to Camp 'Getting Laid,'" I said.

"It wasn't only about that," she insisted. "I learned a lot about..."

"Pop music? Makeup? The fine art of hanging out?" I prompted.

"Come on, was it that unstructured?" she asked.

"I remember hours on end listening to *Frampton Comes Alive* and *Breakfast in America*, and long lines at the mirror to use the blow dryer. It was hard to convince the rest of you to go to activities, especially down at the waterfront."

"That lake was cold and full of seaweed. Peter says they've put in a heated pool!"

"Incredible. Kids today, they have no idea," I said.

"So where did you send yours, if they didn't go to Adelaide?"

"Abby went to day camp, and then high school programs at the local college. We sent Benjy to a sports sleepaway camp, because all the boys in his class were going. He hated it. Came home after two weeks." I shrugged. "He was never much of a joiner. He was better off taking art classes."

Jodi laughed to herself. "Did Roger really call it 'Getting Laid'?"

"Yeah." I laughed too. "I never had boyfriends, but the rest of you..."

"That's not true. The last summer, you went out with Randy Morton."

"For, like, five minutes. Okay, two days. What does 'going out' mean at summer camp, anyway?"

She shrugged. "There's nowhere to go, you just hang out, maybe go behind the Photography bunk and fool around. You know how it is at camp. A day feels like a week, a week is like a month. If you'd gone out with someone for the entire summer, it would have been like a marriage."

"Who were you going with that summer?" I asked her.

"Let's see. Teddy Weiss for about five days, and then Stuart Siegel. That lasted almost three weeks. The one I really liked was Ricky Chernow, but he was with Rachel Friedman."

"I haven't heard those names in forever!" I said. "How do you remember all those people?"

"Oh, some of us would get together afterward, at college or on winter break. Like if they took a road trip for a Conference game, they might crash at my sorority house, or vice versa. And later on, of course, people used to contact me when my business was going well. Ricky Chernow called me once and asked if I was interested in investing with him!"

"No kidding," I said. "What did you say?"

"I already had a great broker," she shrugged. "And a boyfriend. Ricky was cute, but he wasn't exactly a genius. I should have at least met him for drinks though." She paused for a moment and seemed to be caught in a reverie, picturing what it would have been like to have an actual date with her teenage crush. It wouldn't have been a meeting of the minds, but he had a great smile.

It struck me that I really didn't know a lot about her dating history, beyond summer camp and the "Dynamic Duo" photo. "Were you ever serious with anyone besides Gary?"

"Sure. I was even engaged a few times."

"A *few* times?" I asked. "As in more than two?"

"Three," she said. "Well, technically just twice. There was one, early on, that never got to the formal proposal stage. He said, 'Maybe we should talk about getting married,' but then things kind of fizzled."

"And does Gary count as one of the other two?"

"Gary and I never got there either," she confessed. "It started to seem like a merger. I was talking about bringing lawyers and prenups into the picture, so he got skittish. That was the beginning of the end. That, and him killing the company," she said. She started playing with her bendy straw.

"Do you miss him?" I asked.

"Not really. Not any more. I always felt like I was waiting for the other shoe to drop. I wasn't pretty enough, or young enough—something was bound to ruin it. I never truly felt like I could exhale around him—I mean, I gave him my company to run, but I didn't actually believe that he would make a good husband. And he definitely wasn't cut out to be a father. I don't know," Jodi sighed. "Maybe I missed my chance. The first guy was probably the right one, it was just bad timing."

"What happened?" I asked. "Was he a college boyfriend?"

"Yep, we started dating during sophomore year," she said. "Mike Belkin. He was from Highland Park. I used to go home with him for Jewish holidays—Rosh Hashanah, Passover. He had a really nice family."

"So why'd you break up?" I asked.

"I dunno. I guess I thought we couldn't possibly be right for each other because we weren't fully established. I mean, I was going to have an important business career, and he was going on to medical school, and it seemed crazy to think we'd found the right person when we were only nineteen."

I decided not to mention that I'd been that same age when I met Roger. I remembered that some of *our* classmates told us that we were insane to settle down at that age. Fortunately, we hadn't listened.

"Did you dump him?" I asked.

"Yeah," she said. "He's the one who said, 'Maybe we should talk about getting married.' It was senior year, and he said his uncle knew a jeweler on Wabash Avenue. It freaked me out."

Suddenly she jumped up. "What time is it?"

"About ten after three."

"What? How did that happen?" She looked very upset.

"Have you got a date or something? What's the problem?"

"Oh, I've got to get going. I just—I have to go."

She was flustered, digging in her bag for her keys and cell phone. "I'm sorry, I lost track of time. See you!"

I'd never seen her so jittery. I yelled after her as she ran to the driveway. "Okay," I said. "See you!"

CHAPTER 14

It was Tuesday, time for our usual date, but for once I was going to meet Jodi at her mother's condo. Jodi had an eye exam with Peter at noon, but she needed to stop by and help with some of the residual estate bookkeeping. She warned me that she would be chained to her mother's dinette set, swamped with paperwork.

As I walked through the apartment, I noticed a pile of DVDs sitting on the coffee table in the living alcove. "Your mother's watching *Mad Men*?" I asked.

"Oh, yeah. She must have been on another planet the first time it came around. A few months ago, she was in a doctor's office and saw John Slattery and Jon Hamm on the cover of some magazine, and that was it."

Her mother came in from the kitchen. She saw that I was interested in the show and began regaling me with personal anecdotes to prove how accurate it was.

"Listen, I worked on Madison Avenue before I got married. What happened to Peggy—getting pregnant and giving away the baby—that happened to one of my friends. It could have been me: a lot of those men were cheating on their wives."

She went on to tell me that I should warn my daughter, Abby, not to date any of the men she might meet at work. "Look at Peggy. She was with Pete, and then Duck, and now that Ted Shaw."

"Chaough," I said.

"Still. She kept going back to the same well, dating men she worked with. Terrible idea. Never works out."

It occurred to me that Jodi was a real-life example too, with Gary Blenhart, but why remind Mrs. Albert? I just nodded.

"After all, Jodi, how many times did you hear your dad say, 'Don't mix business with pleasure'?"

"You mean, 'Don't shit where you eat,' Ma? He said it plenty of times. Especially about Gary." Jodi looked up from the documents and smiled at me. "Dad loved the concise statements. 'Focus on the deal.' 'Better to underpromise.' 'Get it in writing.'"

I counted out syllables on my fingers. "It sounds like haiku," I said. "Life lessons condensed." I turned back to Jodi's mom. "So, Mrs. Albert, what's it like living in a smaller place? Do you miss your house?"

"Would you stop it with the 'Mrs. Albert' already? Call me Carol." I looked back at Jodi, who shrugged.

"I don't miss the hassles. I don't miss the icy driveway and steps. And I definitely don't miss the wasp nests or weeding the garden. I do miss when the kids were little, but honestly, the house itself…it was getting too quiet, without Alan, and then Peter and Nancy wanted to be in that school district and it just made sense. So here I am." She raised her coffee cup at me.

"I'm sure you see my mother once in a while. She's just around the corner and you know that I'm only about ten minutes away," I said. "And if Jodi ever gives up the City and moves back here…"

"We could be neighbors, dear," Carol enthused.

Jodi snorted. "I'm sure Dad would have had something pithy to say about that!"

"A little Robert Frost, maybe," I offered. "'Good fences make good neighbors'?"

Jodi didn't seem as enthusiastic about the prospect. "An hour away is close enough, I think. Besides, Ma, aren't you afraid that I'm going to find out about all your secret goings-on?"

"Oh, sure," said Carol. "I've got boyfriends lined up around the block." I flinched involuntarily. I saw that Carol noticed out of the corner of her eye.

"But you like your privacy!" Jodi insisted.

"That's true," said Carol. "I gave the house to Peter on purpose."

Jodi nodded. "And I think maybe you don't want people to know exactly how old you are, either. Having a daughter my age kind of blows your cover, don't you think?"

Carol just smiled. "You don't think some of these ladies were married and pregnant by eighteen? Or pregnant and *then* married? It was a different world back then, I'm telling you." She gestured toward the DVDs. "Just because I went to work before getting married…"

Jodi looked at her watch. "Whoops! Don't want to keep Peter waiting!" she said. "Gotta go. I'll check in with you later, Ma," she said.

"Are you leaving now too?" Carol asked me.

I told her I might stick around for a few minutes, if that was okay. She smiled. "Go right ahead. Let me get you some more coffee."

Jodi seemed a bit confused as she picked up her purse. "I guess I'll check in with *you* too."

I nodded as we watched her leave. Carol said, "Tell Peter to drop those boxes by, I'll be home all day."

"No problem, Ma," said Jodi, and headed out the door.

We'd never spent a lot of time together, Carol and I. I remembered her being in my living room, first to play bridge and mah jongg, and later for shiva, but that was the extent of our interaction.

She seemed interesting enough, and her stories were pretty funny. Even though she had only been living in the Pines for about six months, I thought she might know some of the inside gossip. She'd seen me flinch, and when I volunteered to stick around, she had her antennae up. She knew my secret agenda.

"You want to know about Marty and your mom, don't you?"

"Not especially," I said, playing it cool. "I figured she would tell me if she thought it was important. It's none of my business." And it *wasn't*, but if Carol felt like talking, I wasn't going to stop her.

"To be honest, I mostly saw them together when I first moved in, over the winter. She seemed happy. I don't know that she was head-over-heels...she certainly never talked about giving up her unit or anything...but they looked like they enjoyed each other's company."

I nodded. "So you think it was mutual."

"Oh, absolutely. Back in the winter. But I've known Marty for years. He was a client of Alan's. In fact, Alan did most of his legal work...except for his divorces. I guess he wanted

Alan to respect him, so he kept that side of his life separate from their business relationship, if you know what I mean."

"There was some messy stuff, huh?" I asked.

"When his first wife left him, he had to sell off two of his record stores just to cover the alimony. He must have done something pretty bad to have to pay her so much." Carol seemed to know about all kinds of skeletons in Marty's closet.

"Child support, I imagine," I prompted.

"He didn't have any kids. Not with her, or with the other two wives, either. Marty's not exactly a family kind of guy. Maybe your mother saw that. She just didn't seem that enthusiastic about him, the longer they dated, at least as far as I noticed. He got louder, she got quieter."

I gave her a nod and a brief "Hmm." Kind of runs in the family, that quiet observational style. I figured she would just keep talking as long as I gave short, supportive responses.

"I wouldn't be surprised if he's tapped out, paying three alimonies," she added.

If Marty was a gold digger, or whatever the male equivalent would be, then he was definitely wasting his time with my mother. She'd been a smart investor, and she wasn't going to squander her savings on some guy who...? I tried to picture him and just couldn't. I kept imagining the kind of guy Marty must have been thirty or so years ago, when my mom was first widowed. Maybe he was one of those swinger types looking for younger women, with a perm and a gold chain around his neck. By now he would be bald or have a comb-over, with lots of sun spots, and he'd wear dark sunglasses—not to be cool, but to protect his eyes after cataract surgery.

"I can't place him," I admitted. "When you see him, point him out to me, okay?"

She nodded. "You know, I can see wanting a little company every now and then, but I think your mom is better off without him. Anyway, he's Sherry's problem now."

"And what about you?" I asked. "Would you get involved with Marty?"

She laughed. "Oh, never. I know better. He knows better."

"But my mom didn't?" I asked defensively.

"I didn't mean it like that," she said quickly. "I didn't mean your mom was reckless. I think she knew exactly what kind of a person he was, and what he was after. She let herself enjoy the moment. I'm sure she stopped things before he got into her bank account."

Wow. Love and money. There was such intrigue going on in these retirement villas! I shrugged, trying to appear nonchalant. "As I said, none of my business. But thanks for the information, anyway."

"My pleasure," she said. "So did you expect Don Draper to fall to pieces like that, at the Hershey's pitch?" She talked about the television show like it was just another kind of gossip—almost as real, or unreal, as what was going on right in the next building.

CHAPTER 15

That evening, I called Jodi. I wanted to let her know what I'd learned from Carol. The call went straight to voice mail.

"Hey, Jodi, it's me. You won't believe what your mother told me. We were right about my mom and Marty. Call me back, even if it's late!"

I was dying to gossip about my mother. I made Roger turn off the television, so I could share my news with him.

"Mom *was* seeing Marty, from January until only a few weeks ago. Apparently he was interested in her money. Sounds like he didn't fare well, all these years. He has three alimonies to cover."

"You've got to be kidding. Three?"

"Yeah, he's a real playboy...hey, that's pretty accurate. I mean, Hugh Hefner is eighty-something, right? Anyway, Marty had no business sense. He owned a chain of record stores, and then everything went to cassettes and CDs, and then MP3—he sold all his inventory before vinyl became popular again. It wouldn't surprise me if he'd sold answering machines and beepers too," I joked. "A technology museum."

"Come on," said Roger. "Just because he made some poor business decisions, don't pile on..."

I cut him off. "But he's a jerk. From what I heard, both from Carol Albert and the mah jongg ladies, he took up with this other woman, Sherry. The mah jongg ladies made it sound like Sherry stole him away. Carol thinks it's all for the best, that my mom was way too good for him. Even so, it bothers me that anyone would try to take advantage of Mom."

"Does she seem any different to you?" he asked.

"No, not really," I said. Ever since that phone call, Mom and I had maintained close contact, planning the tournament together. In fact, our connection was just about the same as it had always been. We were back to status quo.

"Do you think she has a broken heart?"

"She seems fine. She's acting just like she was before the whole thing started." I shrugged. "Maybe the breakup wasn't so dramatic. Maybe she didn't want him, I don't know. Do you think I should ask her about it?"

Roger shrugged. "It's like with Benjy. You ought to let her initiate the conversation. If she has something she wants to say, she won't hold back."

"Good point," I said. "She basically said as much to me. She said if she felt like talking about it, she'd let me know. You know, I can't imagine the kind of guy who would dump my mother. She's an amazing person!"

"Why do you keep saying that *he* dumped *her*?" Roger asked. "Your mother is fairly self-aware. She's a good judge of character and careful about the company she keeps. I mean, her friends are great people, and you told me she doesn't deal with that other lady, Lois Benson. Your mother has standards. I can't imagine that she would put up with someone if they weren't the right person for her." He continued his line of inquiry. "Didn't Carol say that he wasn't really on her level?"

"That's true," I said. "But the ladies at the Pines made it sound like he had been seduced by Sherry. Made her sound like a hot floozy. Marlene said, 'I wouldn't trust her around *my* husband.'"

"I don't know. It seems like those ladies will gossip about anything," he cautioned. "Sometimes the situation's not nearly as juicy as they make it out to be."

"Then again, sometimes it is." I related the story Carol told me, about how she found her unit in Parnassus Pines. Carol got the place for such a good price because there was an extremely motivated seller.

"You see, there were these two couples who moved to the Pines, maybe four, five years ago. They'd been friends for a long time. A very long time. Forty years or more.

"It turned out they'd been swapping, back and forth, all those years. Real swingers. They took vacations together. Whenever one husband got transferred to another town, they'd all move…the whole nine yards.

"Right around the time that Alan Albert died, one of the husbands, Eddie, also passed away. The other wife started getting worried that Eddie's widow would get grabby and take her husband, Charlie. She wanted to leave the complex and get as far away from Eddie's widow as possible."

"So Carol bought it from Charlie and his wife?" Roger asked.

"That's what I thought too. Let me finish."

"In the end, they both sold. Eddie's widow did run off with Charlie, and Charlie's wife was left high and dry. She couldn't wait to get out of New Jersey. She's living in La Quinta, California, now, and Charlie and the former Mrs. Eddie are down in Boynton Beach, Florida. About as far apart as possible."

Roger whistled. "Parnassus Pines meets Peyton Place."

Jodi and I had just come back from taking a walk through my neighborhood, and we were both sweating like crazy. She sat at my kitchen table, drinking ice water, while I went through the day's mail. I'd received a check from Parnassus Pines for the most recent class I'd taught, plus a flyer from a South Jersey synagogue announcing an upcoming one-day tournament. It could be a chance to see Lisa again.

I checked my calendar to see whether their event would fit into my schedule. "Oh, too bad—we're going to see Steven and his kids that weekend. Maybe another time," I said regretfully.

"With all your running around teaching mah jongg to these different groups, I would think you would want to try something new for yourself," she said. "Aren't you sick of the game by now?"

"Actually, it's quite the opposite: when I run a tournament or watch all the tables of people who are learning to play, I get envious. It makes me want to play more."

I started to muse out loud. "I wonder if that's how it is for the people who work in casinos. Are they just itching to get off work so that they can gamble? Maybe someone who deals blackjack six or eight hours a day is dying to play slots. I never thought about it before."

"It's a little different for them," she said. "I mean, they're working full-time, and the kinds of games they're looking at involve a lot more money, that's for sure. But yes, you have to figure that they never would have bothered going to a casino employment office unless they already had some interest in gambling."

"I'd love to teach you to play, it would be fun," I said.

She inhaled sharply. "I don't think so. I don't have the patience for it."

"I get it. You've got much better things to do with your evenings, anyway," I said. "Are you dating someone, or what? Whenever I call, you're never around."

"I go out," she said vaguely. "You know...some of those dating services and all."

"Anybody good?" I asked.

"Compared to what?" she said. "Nobody as great as Roger, that's for sure."

"Well, still. If you want to spend more time out here in the 'burbs, learning mah jongg, you know where to find the best teacher."

"I certainly do," she said.

———

An hour later, I was still mulling over her question.

"You know, I often think that it would be great if I could *play* as much as I teach—but then I remember, be careful what you wish for. That's the kind of thinking that got me into large binge sessions like that weekend tournament," I said.

"And how was that?" Jodi asked.

"I was playing nonstop for three days, without a group of friends around. Honestly, most of the time I felt terrible."

"Why don't you start up a new group? Or call up some of those girls from your old one?" she asked.

"I don't think so. Do you remember Ilene and Amy Melvin?" I asked.

Jodi thought for a moment. "Oh. Yeah. No, don't bother. But there must be people our age who are fun and interested in playing."

I told her about the "substitute list" at the synagogue. "Sometimes when people are traveling, a group needs a fourth or fifth person. I guess I could put my name on the list."

"Oh, go for it!" she said. "What have you got to lose?"

CHAPTER 17

The infamous "substitute list" from my Sisterhood was more active than I expected it to be. With people going away for the summer, or at least down the Shore for a week here or there, groups often came up short. I got a phone call after only three days.

It was Michelle Fleischer, a woman about five years younger than Jodi and me. "One of our regular players is going to Europe while her kids are at sleepaway camp. I was wondering if you'd be interested in subbing for her next week."

I gratefully accepted, and listened to the details. Michelle explained that she would be hosting. All I needed to do was bring my card and ten dollars on the following Monday evening. She gave me her address, and I told her I looked forward to playing with her and her friends.

The evening gave me quite an education in how other people play mah jongg. I showed up a few minutes early, and while we waited for the other ladies, Michelle tried to list all the group's table rules for me.

"First of all, we each start with a Joker, because that's always nice to have," she said.

"How can you be sure you'll get a Joker?" I asked.

"Oh, we keep four out of the mixing and just give them out."

Okay, I thought. *I guess none of them likes the jokerless Singles and Pairs hands.* "What else?" I asked.

"You're not allowed to make a pass of three Winds. You have to have at least one other kind of tile. And you can't pass three of the same tile."

I've done that occasionally, I thought. *No pass should be off-limits.* "And?"

"Let's say you only want to pass one in the Optional, and the person across from you wants to pass three. And it's the same with the other two people—one wants one, the other wants three. It doesn't matter *who* you do the Optional with—you can pass with the other person that wants to do three."

"But what if three of the people want to exchange three?" I asked. "What happens then?"

"Hmm. Never thought of that, it usually isn't a problem. Um, what else? We play cold wall—"

"Explain, please?" Some people use the terms "hot" and "cold" wall to cover all kinds of variations on the final part of the game, limiting discards and exposures, so I wanted to know her specific rule.

"On the last wall, you can't call for any discard except your mah jongg tile."

"Okay…" I said.

"And for exchanging Jokers, we play that you can do a reverse."

"What do you mean?" I asked, although I was afraid that I already knew.

"Let's say someone has exposed four Flowers, and you're going for a hand that needs a pair of them. You can use Jokers to trade back for any exposed tile."

"Hmm. All right, then," I said. I'm a real stickler for the formal rules, and in my head, I was horrified, screaming, "*No! No! That's barbaric!*" It was my worst fear—switching back the other way was totally against the original rules, and for me it was like waving garlic in front of a vampire. I tried my best to display no emotion.

While we were waiting, I made a thorough internal assessment of their little modifications. The changes were all in strict violation of the League rules. The only reaction I made aloud was, "This is going to be an interesting game." I wanted to check on one last thing, so I asked, "Is there anything about the fees and doubling that I should know?"

"Oh, yes! I mentioned that we have a ten-dollar pie. We double the value of each hand, and for any wall games, you put a dollar in the kitty. If someone has gone pie, she can pay from the money in the kitty."

A "pie" is a loss limit: what Michelle meant was that each of us begins with ten dollars, and pays the winner of each game between fifty cents and three dollars, depending on which hand she achieves and how she wins it. The amounts are listed on the card. If no one wins a specific game, it's considered that the "Wall" has won, and every player puts a dollar into the kitty. If any player loses all ten dollars and then owes money to a winner, her payment can come out of that kitty. At the end of the night, no one will have lost more than ten dollars, and someone may go home with quite a bit.

"What happens to the kitty at the end of the night?" I asked.

"We carry it over to the next time," she told me.

"Fair enough. I guess I'm up to speed on your rules," I said.

While we waited for the other girls, I asked Michelle how long she'd been playing. "Oh, about three years. Sue Sherwood taught us all to play."

I'd met Sue at Parnassus Pines a few months ago, when she accompanied her mother-in-law to one of the family events in the Clubhouse. Rona Sherwood was a good friend of Lois Benson's. I surmised that Lois taught Rona, who taught Sue, who taught these ladies. Like a bad game of "Telephone," the rules no doubt got messed up somewhere along the line.

"And do you ever play in any other groups or at tournaments?" I asked.

"No, never. You're our first sub, even. I just adore this game. I've already bought three sets of tiles—these are my sparkly pink ones," she said. They were brand-new, and had personalized Jokers with "Michelle" written in fuchsia script.

"They're great," I said. "Very easy to read. Where did you find the other two sets?"

"One was from a garage sale. The racks were kind of banged up and the Joker stickers needed to be replaced but it's vintage, probably from the 1950s. I'm going to get it cleaned up. I bought my other set brand-new, online, but I don't like it as much. It's kind of plain."

I nodded. That was the thing about acquiring mah jongg sets—there were some people who loved the tiles and collected many different styles. Many of the Parnassus Pines ladies were from an earlier generation that was more frugal—one set was good enough. They would use it week after week, even as the paint was fading off the tiles.

"I've got two sets myself," I explained. "I have my grandmother's set—from my dad's mom, I mean. The problem is that you can always tell when a Joker's coming, since it's a slightly different color, so I also bought a plain vanilla set that I use for regular games."

Michelle nodded as the bell rang. Sue was at the door. Kayla came soon after. We sat down to play in Michelle's den. She had some lovely Asian-inspired decorations in the room, and had set up the table beautifully, with small snack tables on two of the corners. She had put out drinks and coasters, as well as a few different kinds of nibbling foods: pretzels, popcorn, peanuts, and raisins.

I sat across from Michelle, and the other girls took their seats. As hostess, Michelle was the first East. She passed out four Jokers—one to each of us—and then rolled two dice to break the East wall.

For the entire evening, I kept my mouth shut and let their rules be the law of the land. I tried to adjust quickly to all the new regulations. For instance, that business of having at least one Joker every time was a strange way to begin a game. It certainly opened up some possibilities, but as soon as that Joker was used to make an exposure, it was fair game for anyone else to take.

I was surprised to find out just how easy it was to incorporate their "reverse Joker" rule. I figured out all sorts of ways to use it: trading Jokers back for Soaps or Flowers, or to complete any pair. Since I wasn't at all afraid of the Singles and Pairs hands, it was great for me to be able to get rid of Jokers in exchange for the tiles that I needed. Usually difficult hands to make, these Singles and Pairs options had the highest payoffs on the official card.

As the night wore on, I hated to take advantage of their

generosity…well, no, I didn't. The ladies were accustomed to the ten-dollar pie. It was a much higher amount than I ordinarily play for, but I had no intention of reaching the loss limit, or of losing, period. As a guest, I accepted the table rules that they established, but I had a lot more experience with the game than any of them so I knew how to manipulate their table rules. Personally, I'd never use any of those variations in my own game—I appreciate the clarity and structure of the original game. It was a successful night and I ended up with an additional twenty-two dollars.

I tried calling Jodi to tell her how I'd won big, but she didn't pick up. "It's me," I said to voice mail. "Rolling in dimes and quarters. I guess I'll tell you about it at lunch."

The next day, I recounted the entire story. "I still want to teach you to play," I said, "but not with those absurd rules."

"I don't think I can afford a hobby like this," she said. "You're pretty merciless."

I remembered how lopsided my victories had been and said, "Some of the table rules they came up with were crazy. I don't think they thought them out, so I was using all the loopholes."

"Were they nice people?" she asked. "You told me you were trying to find a new group to play with."

"I suppose they were. Michelle was very friendly. I don't know, I didn't make much small talk. I came to play, not to make friends."

"I'm not sure they're going to ask you back." She paused. "It doesn't sound like you're ready for a social game."

"Not with them, their rules were ridiculous. I promise it

would be different for you. I would teach you the real rules and we wouldn't have all those extra things going on."

"Not interested, sorry," she said. "You're going to have to find another pigeon."

It was only July, and already my mother was finding that the tournament planning was too much work for her to handle. She decided the committee needed a third member.

"But only three of us," she swore. "If we make it any bigger, we'll never get anything done."

"I hear you," I said. "I hate committees, and those endless meetings. Nothing ever gets accomplished except scheduling another meeting for the following month."

"You're my kid, all right. You'd rather take an idea and run with it—see your project through, from start to finish. That's why I picked you to be the mah jongg instructor. I knew you could handle it."

I felt myself glowing. What can I say, even after fifty years I still bask in my mother's approval. It felt good to hear that she was proud of me.

"So who do you have in mind for the third?" I asked her.

"I was thinking of Carol Albert," she said.

"Really? I guess she used to play, way back when," I said. I figured that Mom just wanted to get Carol connected, knowing that she was relatively new to the neighborhood.

"I think she might be good," Mom said. "Let's have her come over next week."

———

Around this time, something unexpected came to light having to do with Benjy. We hadn't pushed him into a summer job, especially with the scholarship waiting for him, so he had a lot of free time on his hands.

Even over the summer, he was still cruising around on his own. He reliably gave me updates as to when he would be home, but never told me what it was that he was actually doing.

I finally confronted him, asking him point-blank when he got home at about 8:15 on a Saturday evening. He'd spent the day with my mother.

"What could you two have found to keep yourselves so busy?" I wondered.

"Oh, we had a good time. We hit an estate sale and some of the antiques shops up in Sussex County," he said. "Carol wanted to see if there was any original Fiestaware. I'm helping her complete her collection."

"Carol? As in Carol Albert?"

"Oh. Yeah." He looked embarrassed, as if I'd caught him doing something wrong.

"Have you seen her often?" I asked. He winced.

"Out with it, kid."

Benjy told me that he'd known Carol for years, from synagogue, and that she had moved into Parnassus Pines due to my mom's insistence.

"I had no idea that they were so close. It's certainly better for her to keep company with Carol than to be dating Marty," I reasoned.

For several months, it seemed that Benjy's visits with his grandmother had turned into a party of three.

"They're so happy that you and Jodi are hanging out. That was *my* idea first," he said proudly.

"What are you talking about? I ran into Jodi at Citi Field, totally by accident."

"Yup," said Benjy. "It was only a matter of time."

Apparently we'd been "set up." My mother didn't like that I had no friends my age. Benjy was worried that I'd be lonely once he left for college. Carol had been concerned about Jodi ever since she stepped down from being CEO—and even more so since Gary wrecked the company and left her. They'd all been so pleased to push the two of us together.

"So, I didn't just happen to see Jodi?"

"You're right, the Mets thing was completely by accident. After that, Jodi mentioned to Carol that she'd run into you, and then Carol told us about it one afternoon. I came up with a way to organize a formal thing. Carol and Grandma invited you and Jodi over on the same day, so that you'd both be in the parking lot around the same time. It was a calculated plan," he added, doing his best evil scientist voice.

I suddenly remembered my mother's comment: "Maybe you should talk to her." She'd been pretty straightforward about it.

"Well, your plan seems to be working," I said. "Thank you."

"One more thing," he said. "Carol wants to know why Jodi never answers the phone in the evenings. She's tried to get ahold of her, and whenever it's past five p.m., she's completely cut off. What's up with that?"

"Come on. Carol wants me to be friends with Jodi, but the truth is she just wants me to spy on her? I don't think so," I said. "Maybe her daughter just has an active social life."

"Yeah, I figured you'd feel that way," said Benjy. "But if you do find anything out, Carol would like to know. Just saying."

I told him I'd take it under advisement. I also said that Carol was overthinking things. It was probably just a coincidence. The evenings that Carol called, she got no answer. And the evenings that I called, I got no answer. I remembered how Jodi had dashed out, late, on more than one occasion—it certainly seemed that there was something very important going on in the City every night.

After Benjy went upstairs, I put in a call to my mother. "So you and your BFF, Carol Albert, are in the matchmaking business now?"

"What are you talking about?" she asked.

"Putting Jodi and me together—it was your idea to get us to be friends again?"

"It was a good idea," she said. "You both seem a lot happier these days."

"That's true," I admitted. "So speaking of interfering in other people's lives..."

"Excuse me?" Mom obviously didn't appreciate the characterization. "Interfering?"

"I just have a few questions. Mainly about you and Marty Wolf."

How could she think I would never ask about this? She didn't seem surprised to hear his name, but still tried to interrupt me. "Nothing happened, really. I was just going around with him for a few months."

"Don't worry, Mom. I don't need intimate details. I just want to know whose idea it was to end it."

"Oh. Mine, *please*," she said. "Have you met him?"

"No, actually," I said. "I wouldn't know him if I saw him."

"He's a sweet, nebbishy guy. Not the brightest bulb. But he

ended up on his feet. He's been dating another woman here for a few months now."

"Oh, Sherry? Yeah, I heard about her," I said. "Nothing escapes the gossip train at Parnassus Pines."

CHAPTER 19

"Mom was never interested in dating," I said to Roger. "She even said, 'Why would I want to take care of an old man?'"

It was August, two months since I had learned about the breakup, yet I was still beating that dead horse. It just didn't make sense to me that my mother would take up with a guy who didn't deserve her. Her relationship with Marty had come as such a surprise to me—it had never occurred to me that, after all these years, she was looking for a male companion.

"If the money part is true, then Marty definitely initiated things. Maybe Mom just got caught up in the attention until she grew tired of it," Roger reasoned.

With Marty out of the picture, Mom had reverted back to her usual part-time escort, Uncle Fred. We were having a combined birthday, graduation, and going-away barbecue for Benjy, and Uncle Fred drove down from Westchester to be part of the festivities. Abby and her boyfriend, Ethan, were there, of course, and I invited Benjy's other "antiquing buddy," Carol, who brought Jodi. Roger's parents came down to us from Hartford, and that was it: another small and intimate gathering.

Benjy was helping me set up the room. "So have you got everything you need for Parsons?" I asked.

"Sure, Grandma and Carol and I have been doing lots of shopping," he said. "My dorm's going to look great."

That story I'd spun to my students was all too true—my baby didn't need me anymore. When Jodi arrived, I started pouting about it.

"Talia, it's time to face facts. He's been independent for a long time," said Jodi. "Honestly—once he started driving, how often did he need your help?"

"Okay, I admit it. I was *hoping* he still needed me," I told her.

"Enjoy the freedom. You'll be babysitting for Abby's kids in no time," said Carol.

Abby didn't find this funny. She hadn't warmed up to Carol yet, and treated her with her usual "you-don't-know-me" scowl. "I don't see that happening anytime soon," she said.

Ethan had been working as a summer associate at a big Wall Street law firm, but he was living with his parents for the summer and commuting in, in order to save money. Abby was also living at home, with us, but she was doing nonprofit work, helping to file restraining orders for residents of battered women's shelters throughout New Jersey. They had spent the majority of their nonworking time hanging out at our house.

"Whenever you're ready, I'm ready," I told her. "I'm sure I remember how to change a diaper."

I, too, was given a cold, angry stare by Abby. She was not in the mood to discuss such topics.

I saw that Roger's parents were chatting with Carol and my mother, so I went over to talk with my Uncle Fred. At the seder, he had mentioned that he was in the process of winding down his dental practice.

"Are you still working?" I asked. "Have you given up the practice yet?"

"I'm only going in once or twice a week," he told me. "I've passed most of the administrative headaches off to Dr. Brinkman. I also gave him all of my younger patients. He brought in some new equipment, has lots more kid-oriented stuff in the waiting room. He's changed the family practice model I used to have. It's almost exclusively a pediatric dental practice, not many adult patients anymore."

I nodded. "So did my mom tell you about her boyfriend?"

He looked at me, a little surprised. Uncle Fred liked to tease Mom, but he would never gossip about her behind her back.

"Come on, I don't need to know what my sister's up to, she's a big girl."

"No, I'm just curious. She didn't tell *me* anything," I confessed. "I thought she might have mentioned it to you."

"It's not my business," he said. He seemed caught off guard, though, at the idea of her being involved with someone. "She really loved your dad. You see how long she waited before she ever even thought about dating. Some people only find love once, you know?"

"I don't think it was love," I said, "and besides, it's over. She didn't even tell me about it herself. I had to hear about it on the streets! Anyway, he was some playboy. He has a string of girlfriends. I have no idea why he picked Mom."

"Your mother's nice-looking, you know that. Of course, she's not a glamour girl or anything..." He paused to consider the situation. "Was he out for her money, do you think?"

We both laughed. "No wonder it didn't last very long," he said. "A fortune hunter and Franny. I just can't see it."

"I never even met the guy," I confessed. "I picture him like Christian Bale in *American Hustle*, with a comb-over and a paunch, but he's even older than that."

"Sansabelt slacks," said Uncle Fred. "White shoes. Ah, well. We're all getting older. Nothing we can do about it."

"Not you, Uncle Fred. You never age. So who are you dating these days?"

He looked at me with mock surprise. "*Moi*? Paris Hilton wasn't interested, so now I'm thinking of going after whichever Kardashian will have me."

"That's a great idea. Do they spend a lot of time up in Mount Kisco?"

He shook his head. "You know me. I can't seem to find the right girl," he said. "But I'm available for Franny whenever she needs me."

"Thank you for that," I said. "She always says, you're a great dance partner."

"Maybe we'll have another occasion to dance soon," he said, nodding his head toward Ethan and Abby.

"If she doesn't kill him first," I said. "I don't know why he puts up with all her arguing."

"You don't have to know why. It obviously works for them. Who can guess what makes any two people fall in love?" he mused.

chapter 20

It was about 8:30, and the graduation barbecue was winding down. I put Abby and Ethan in charge of the cleanup. I kissed Roger's parents and Uncle Fred goodbye, and waved as each drove away.

My mother, Carol, and Jodi were sitting out on the patio, being entertained by Benjy. Roger and I had an opportunity to just stand back and breathe.

"I can't believe he's leaving the nest," I said. "I never thought I'd see the day."

"Want to recite the *Shehecheyanu*?" Roger asked.

I smiled. It was a prayer of thanksgiving for having reached an important milestone. The last time we had recited it was at Benjy's bar mitzvah. "Sure."

We said it, together: "Baruch atah Adoshem, elokeinu melekh ha'olam, shehecheyanu, v'kiyimanu, v'higiyanu, l'azman hazeh." *Blessed are you, Lord our God, King of the Universe, who has granted us life, sustained us, and enabled us to reach this occasion.*

We moved into the hallway where we could get a peek at Ethan and Abby sharing kitchen duties. Ethan was telling her about his job, and what it felt like to have to commute every day into New York.

"It's like becoming a different person," he said. "I feel like I'm putting on a suit of armor or something every morning, and it's horrible dealing with the crowded bus. I don't know how people do it."

"My grandpa did it for twenty years and it killed him," Abby said. "I don't ever want to work in Manhattan."

I paused for a moment, stunned. I looked up at Roger. "Wow. Does she really believe that?" I asked him.

"Sounds like it," he agreed. "Where do you think she got that idea?"

"I don't know. I never put it in those terms. Maybe that's what my mom has told her. Maybe she interpreted it herself. I know she's got strong opinions, but that's a harsh thing to say, even for her. She never knew my father. You didn't either," I admitted. "I'm sure he would have been proud of her, but I don't think he would want her to be so angry all the time."

I moved out to the deck, where Carol, Benjy, and my mom were chatting and laughing. I was very curious to hear my mother's take on Abby's statement, but I knew that now wasn't a good time to talk about it. It was sure to ruin my mother's mood completely. I made a mental note to bring up the topic at another time.

Jodi was sitting off to the side, and I realized she wasn't saying much. She stood up and said, "It's getting late and I'm really wiped out. Ma, is it okay if I stay over with you?"

This caught Carol by surprise. I had never seen Jodi look so exhausted. I suddenly realized that I'd never seen her at this hour of the day. She was always back in the City, out of New Jersey by late afternoon. She was like Cinderella from a different time zone: 5 p.m. instead of midnight.

She looked very weak, and I said, "Do you need me to drive?"

"Don't be silly," said Carol. "I can get us home. Come on, kiddo." I noticed that she looked strong, and somehow pleased that her daughter was willing to show some vulnerability. "I'll get us fresh bagels in the morning."

Benjy headed up to his room. Mom wanted to go with the Alberts back to Parnassus Pines, but I indicated that she should stick around. We both waved goodbye as Carol drove off with Jodi.

We came back into the house. "So?" she asked. I gestured to the couch. I had lots of different topics that I could bring up, but it wasn't the right time to talk about Dad, and I honestly couldn't care less about Marty at that moment. I went for a third topic that I knew wouldn't upset my mother.

"Uncle Fred was being extremely sentimental tonight," I said. "I realized I don't know much about his life, other than that he's your twin brother, a dentist, and a really good dancer."

She nodded. "He was a great dancer. I don't know that either of us is up for that anymore, but I'm lucky that I have him."

"Well, why do you?" I asked. "I mean, why isn't he married? He was a good-looking guy, had a nice career. Why didn't he ever get married?"

"He did."

"What?! You never told me that!" I said. "I've known him all my life. How could you never tell me he was married? Who was she? What happened to her?" I nearly pounced on her with questions.

"I have no idea what happened to her," said my mother, "and I have to say I haven't even thought of her since you were a baby. Uch, such a woman." She was full of disdain at the mere thought.

"Did they get divorced? Tell me!" Suddenly there was a great family secret, and I was dying to hear it.

"Fred doesn't like to talk about it," she confessed. "It happened quickly; it ended quickly. We don't even have any wedding pictures. Back then, professional photo albums took about eight months, and by that time they were already divorced!"

I was shocked. "What kind of a girl—Uncle Fred was married *and* divorced within a year? I guess that's why you and Grandma never mentioned it, but geez, it must have scarred him. If it was when I was a baby, you would think he would have gotten over it and remarried by now."

"I guess he never met anyone special," she said.

"He was talking awfully sentimentally tonight," I told her again. "I never heard him talk about love like that before. Even at my wedding—I mean, he gave me away, but he never made a speech or anything. Tonight, he spoke very sweetly about Abby and Ethan. He said how some people only find love once, and about how none of us could guess what made them fall in love."

My mother looked surprised. "That *is* pretty sentimental, for Fred. 'Some people only find love once.' What made him say that, I wonder?"

I blushed, realizing that his remark was about my parents. "To be honest, I was telling him a little about you and Marty, and he said he didn't think Marty was the right guy for you. He made it sound like you and Dad were mated for life, and that no one else could ever live up to that."

My mom sat up a little straighter. "I think that's true, actually," she said quietly. "I couldn't love anyone as much as I loved your dad. I just didn't realize Fred thought that way too."

"It must run in the family," I said.

chapter 21

"I just called Carol's house," I announced to Roger. "Jodi is still asleep. She told Carol last night that she was having a migraine."

"Oh. She didn't look well," he said. "Maybe that wild lifestyle is catching up to her." We sometimes speculated that she dated up a storm, back in the City. It would explain why she'd had to rush back that afternoon, and why she never returned calls at night. "Does she get migraines a lot?"

"I don't know. She's never mentioned them before," I replied, "but remember, I've only seen her during the day. Do they tend to get worse at night?"

We were bringing Abby back to Ithaca for her second year of law school. We'd stopped for an early lunch at our usual place, Abe's Deli in Scranton.

"One of my roommates got migraines sometimes," Abby said. "It didn't matter what time of day. A lot of it was brought on by stress. Too much studying."

"I think it depends on the person," Roger said. "Some people get them in the morning."

"Does anyone in your lab do migraine research?" I asked. "Maybe we know someone who can help her."

"No, we're always focused on infectious diseases. I could ask around, though," he said.

"Hmm. Maybe she should go see a neurologist," I said.

"I think she already does, Mom," said Abby. "She's a grown woman, she's probably had them before."

We were able to get all of Abby's things unloaded and

moved into her apartment quickly. On the way home, I got a text from Jodi: "Back home now and feeling better. Talk to you tomorrow." There was also a voice mail message on our home phone.

I had to play it back a second time to figure it out. The voice wasn't familiar. The speaker sounded raspy, making snuffling sounds between phrases.

"Hi (*sniff*) Talia. My name is Sherry Kandel. (*sniff*) I'm wondering (*sniff*)...I mean, I'm looking for a mah jongg instructor. (*sniff*) Do you ever give a *private* lesson?" Her voice got higher at the word "private," as if she were begging. She sounded so pathetic on the phone that I felt compelled to call her back immediately.

"Sherry, hi. It's Talia Welt."

"Talia, thank you for calling back. Did you understand my message?"

"Yes, you said you're looking for private lessons. Do you mean for you and a group of friends?"

"Oh. No. Not exactly," she said. "By private, I meant just you and me. Can you do that?"

"Where are you located?" I asked. I wasn't going to travel halfway across the state.

"I'm in Parnassus Pines. Did I forget to say that in the message?" she asked. "That's how I got your number."

Just as there was more than one Fran, there were probably three or four Sherrys in the development, but I had a pretty good hunch that she was *that* Sherry, the one dating Marty Wolf. I tried to picture this infamous woman. I'd never seen her or said a word to her. The way I'd heard people talk about her, she sounded like Elizabeth Taylor and

Marilyn Monroe all rolled into one—some kind of voluptuous, home-wrecking seductress. How much of a vamp could she still be, pushing 70?

"Sherry, I think I need to meet with you before I can commit to anything. Could we get together tomorrow morning and discuss options?"

She hesitated. "Okay. Sure. I'm at 81 Troy Terrace."

"How's 10 a.m.?"

"Fine. See you then."

I hung up the phone, and went in to talk to Roger.

"You'll never guess who I'm tutoring, tomorrow," I said.

"Yep. You're right. I'm not even going to try," he said. "Just please tell me."

"Sherry Kandel."

"Wouldn't have guessed. Who, exactly, is that?"

"I think she's the same Sherry who is dating Marty," I said. "I've heard all these things. One woman said she wouldn't trust Sherry around her husband…a few weeks ago, another student of mine said she dresses too provocatively."

"Really?" asked Roger. "What's provocative for a seventy year old?"

"My mom never said a word about her. She's never been bitter about the whole thing with Marty. I don't know, I'm going to take my tack from Mom. If she bears no ill will toward Sherry, then I'm going to treat her like any other lady at the Pines."

Roger nodded. "Sounds fair to me. Sherry probably had nothing to do with the breakup, especially if your mom didn't want Marty in the first place. Sherry's just an innocent bystander."

"That's what I thought," I agreed. "But…do you think she knows people don't like her? Do you think she knows I'm Fran Klein's daughter?"

"I have no idea, honey," he said. "Why don't you meet her tomorrow and find out?"

I stewed on it for a little longer. I was pretty sure that Sherry *didn't* know that Fran Klein was my mom. In hindsight, I don't think she would have reached out to me, if she had…she might have expected me to be like the ladies in Parnassus Pines, so quick to point fingers and blame her for the breakup. She would have had to be all kinds of stupid to be seeking help and sympathy from the daughter of the woman whom she'd reputedly wronged.

Realizing that she didn't know who I was, I felt a little bit sneaky going to see her. In a way I was just spying, wanting to find out more of the truth in Mom's story. Was she a bimbo, a vacuous beauty, or more of an aggressive man-stealer? Maybe Roger was right, that she really *was* an innocent bystander in this whole situation, just another woman that Marty met.

———

I arrived about five minutes early to Sherry's unit on Troy Terrace. I brought a set of tiles and two copies of the current card.

Except for a friend like Jodi, I don't offer one-on-one lessons too often. Demand is so high that I usually can put a group together, and therefore get more return for the same amount of effort. Even teaching a semi-private group of four players is pretty rare, but I'm happy for that kind of work:

focusing on one table of play, helping each of the players get better. That's actually the best kind of teaching, as far as I'm concerned, but again, with the waitlists going on around town, I can easily get a group of eight or twelve players. Once it gets to four tables, I try to have a co-teacher with me, since I can't focus on so many people at once.

Sherry would be getting my full attention. I didn't know whether she'd played before or we would have to start at square one, but I was ready to give her the best lessons I could.

I rang the buzzer and she came right to the door, cheerful and pleased to see me. She had a dazzling smile. She was petite, about five feet tall, with blue-gray eyes and what we used to call "frosted," curly hair. She was wearing a tennis dress and generally seemed like a throwback to the late 1970s. The fashion and hairstyle worked well on her, but most people didn't go for that look anymore. She struck me as one of the prettiest ladies at Parnassus Pines.

"Talia. Right on time." She ushered me into her foyer area. "Come on in."

Her apartment was set up exactly like my mother's: powder room and closet, living alcove, dining alcove, etc. The couch and end tables were even identical to Mom's. I imagined that the sales office offered an option to purchase a furnished unit, and that I'd find matching love seats and couches all up and down the streets of the Pines.

The biggest difference between Sherry's apartment and the many others I'd seen was the artwork, and particularly the photography, on display. There were some impressive Ansel Adams-style black-and-white nature shots, as well as a few scattered color pictures of Sherry and her late husband. No photos of kids or grandchildren, though.

"Sit down, sit down," she urged. "Would you like a drink? A bottle of water, maybe?"

"That would be great," I answered. She puttered around the kitchen and came out with two bottles of water and coasters.

"So tell me about your game. Have you been playing a long time, or are you just learning?" I asked.

"I knew the game, many years ago, but I never played. I wanted to learn because it's so *popular* here." She smiled at me. "I was hoping you could bring me up to speed."

I opened up my set and started talking about absolute basics: the suits, the number of tiles of each kind, the matching dragons. She caught on quickly. I asked if she'd been a card player, and she said that she and her husband were big gin rummy players. I told her that those concepts would come in handy with mah jongg.

I then moved on to explaining the card. This proved a little trickier. I laid out a few different hands on the table for her, showing her how the tiles corresponded. I knew that some of the Consecutive Runs would be easier for her to grasp, since they were the most like a rummy hand.

After about an hour, her eyes began to glaze over. "I think that's enough for the day," I said. "You've made an excellent start. I can tell you're going to be good at this."

She smiled and said, "The ladies over at the Clubhouse haven't been willing to work with me. They don't want to waste their time with a beginner. It's nice to have a patient teacher. You're so kind to help me like this."

I felt guilty about my secret identity. "Sherry, I need to tell you something that I should have mentioned when I called you back."

"What is it?" she asked. She could see that I was uncomfortable, and it worried her.

"You know I'm Talia Welt. My mom is Fran Klein," I said.

"Okay…?" she said, not understanding.

"I don't know, I'm sorry for putting you on the spot. My mom was dating Marty Wolf a few months ago…maybe he told you about her?"

"Oh! *Fran!* Yes, he said he'd been dating someone else in the Pines, but that it was a while ago and there were no hard feelings. Anyway, I'm not with Marty now either, if that makes you feel any better about it. I hope it doesn't mean you don't want to teach me," she said, looking concerned.

I could see she didn't have a jealous bone in her body, nor did she seem to recognize that the gossips had been hostile to her because of their "loyalty" to my mother. "Of course, I'm happy to teach you! I'm glad you called me. Don't give it a second thought," I told her.

I tried to change the subject by remarking on some of the photos on her wall. "I know Ansel Adams liked the National Parks. I don't recall him doing many beach scenes."

"Oh, no, those are mine!" she said. "I've been an amateur photographer for years."

"Really?" I said. "Wow. They're great."

She took some albums off of the shelf to show me more of her work. Her subjects were mainly nature scenes: some close-ups, some color, but a lot of black-and-white.

"You're very talented," I told her.

"Thank you. So can we get together again next week?" she asked.

We set a date, and I left. I thought about that sniffly message in my voice mail. Maybe she had been crying about her breakup with Marty, or because the mean ladies wouldn't include her in their mah jongg games. Perhaps I had misinterpreted it: maybe she'd only had a cold.

Fall

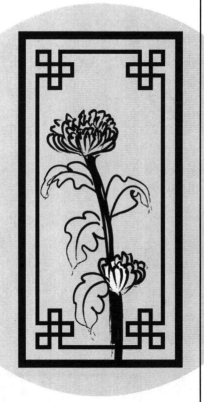

chapter 22

"There you go again, stirring up trouble," said Carol. "I don't know why you want to have Lois Benson on your bad side and why you keep putting your daughter in the line of fire."

My mother played dumb. "I'm just trying to have as many people at this event as possible and Talia's going to help them get ready. I don't see the harm in that."

With the big Parnassus Pines tournament coming, Mom had volunteered my services for a few "quick clinics" in September and October, where I would work with small groups to prepare them for the challenge of a tournament. She wanted every able-bodied mah jongg player to be in the Great Room on Sunday, November sixteenth.

"We're raising money for the Red Cross," she added innocently. "How can they say no?"

It wasn't the charity that was the issue. To some people, the Executive Board had reclaimed yet another region of Lois's empire. She had lost the classes *and* the tournaments. Now all Lois Benson had left were the card room sessions on Mondays and Thursdays.

Mom insisted that it wasn't personal. "This was a decision by the entire Board. It was unanimous that changes needed to be made. We want a more inclusive event and to make sure that all of the charitable funds reach their beneficiary. Remember, Lois never even specified a charity."

Carol nodded, acquiescing. Now very much a part of our tournament committee, she had been given a special assignment. She was still new to the development, so there were quite a few people who hadn't met her yet. Her job was to "infiltrate" Monday Morning Mahj and do a little snooping around among the regulars. Carol found that Lois Benson hadn't endorsed our event. In fact, she was actively discouraging her little gang from participating.

"I don't know about the catering...Fran Klein's trying to raise money, so I'm sure she'll be cutting corners," Lois had been overheard saying. "And only having *three* cash prizes? I don't think she knows how to run a tournament." This was, of course, patently untrue—my mother had thrown several excellent tournaments at our synagogue, in years past, but some of Lois's loyalists wouldn't dare question their leader.

"What are *you* planning to do?" Carol asked, one Thursday morning in September. She was sitting at a table with three other ladies, all relatively new to the Pines.

"Oh, I don't play in tournaments," said the first, Lily. "Our group just plays for fun." She gestured toward the other two ladies at the table, Trish and Annalee. "We've been playing mah jongg together for about fifteen years, along with another gal named Madeleine."

"I happen to know that there's a woman who teaches players how to get ready for tournaments," said Carol. "You should call her, she'll come to you! And invite Madeleine!"

———

The following Wednesday morning, I schlepped over to Lily Sherman's unit—67 Dionysus Drive. She and the other ladies had been playing together since before they lived in Parnassus Pines. One by one, they had downsized from larger homes, and the main reason they'd all ended up in the same development was because of the strong "mahj friend-ship" that had formed.

They seemed like a lovely group, and they were quite en-thusiastic about learning something new. We all arrived at around the same time, pulling into the small Visitor Lot in the middle of Lily's block.

As I walked into her condo, I noticed it was configured like many of the others in the neighborhood. She had moved the coffee table away from the couch in the living room alcove, and in its place had set up a card table and chairs. As the fifth, nonsitting player, I wanted to walk around, observ-ing each of the four players' hands. Unfortunately, the quar-ters were a little tight for me to gracefully make the circuit. I had to push the couch about two feet, right up against the wall, in order to make space for myself.

Lily put out some raisins and nuts, and said, "I've got cof-fee brewing. Go ahead and help yourselves." The others went into the kitchen area to get themselves properly caffeinated; I was sticking to my bottle of water.

I looked at her wall display—wedding photos of her chil-dren, a collage with pictures of her grandchildren. There was a great 16 x 20 portrait of her and her husband in Ad-irondack chairs, holding up cocktail glasses as a toast. It was taken near sunset on some beach, and looked like a well-deserved retirement celebration. For a moment, I thought wistfully of my dad.

The ladies bustled back to the table. I explained, as they settled into their seats, that I was going to observe their typ-ical style of play for a hand or two, and then I would give them some feedback.

"Just to confirm—your main goal today is to get ready for a tournament, is that correct?" I asked. They all nodded. "So we'll talk about rules and strategy, but first I want to see what level of play you're at."

Trish rolled a six and broke the wall accordingly. Everyone picked up their own little stacks of tiles and set them up on their racks. The first real problem came at the beginning of the Charleston.

"Too bad this set doesn't come with any Jokers," said Annalee. "Sure wish it did."

Obviously they were playing with a standard American mah jongg tile set, complete with eight Jokers, but Annalee was complaining because she didn't have any on her rack. The other ladies kvetched about their own equally bad tiles. I considered it to be typical mah jongg table talk.

What I wasn't expecting to hear was the specificity of their discussion. "I need odds," said Lily. "Don't anyone give me even tiles."

"Is somebody collecting the Winds?" asked Madeleine. "I have an East and I don't need it."

Are you seriously discussing your tiles during the Charleston? I thought. I decided to hold my tongue and wait until the entire game was over before correcting them.

"Ugh," said Annalee. "I have no idea what to do with these. What do you think?" She showed me her tiles. They weren't the worst I'd ever seen, but without Jokers, it was true that she had a long way to go to win.

I felt like I should help them manage their high expectations. "One thing I want to remind all of you—you probably only should expect to win 20 percent of the time. If you know what hand to play, and come close, that's really good, but you can't expect that you will always win. You should be used to that by now, since you play every week."

Lily nodded her head. "None of us wins every single time, it's true."

After the Charleston ended, Madeleine put out two tiles, face down. "What's that?" I asked.

"For the mush," she said. She was referring to an additional blind exchange of unwanted tiles. This was a table rule, strictly illegal according to the League and tournament rules, and I shook my head vigorously.

"There is no such thing in tournament rules. Right after the optional, you start the game. No mush."

They looked disappointed, but started the game. Trish, as East, threw out a Four Bam. I watched as they picked and threw, sometimes calling for exposures. Lily discarded a tile and then said, "No, wait—I want to keep it."

"Sorry, Lily, once you name it or put it down, it's a discard," I told her. She pouted briefly.

Later, when Annalee discarded a Three Bam that could have been exchanged for Lily's exposed joker, the other ladies pointed out her mistake. "You're right," she said. She took back the Three Bam and made the exchange.

I cleared my throat. "Also illegal in tournaments. Once it's thrown, it's thrown. You can't take it back."

Annalee was even more upset at my strictness than Lily had been. Trish spoke up on her behalf. "She never gets Jokers, can't she just keep it?"

I explained that in a tournament, no one would give her a second chance. "Besides, Annalee, now that you know to look at all the exposures before you discard, you'll be more alert, right? You won't make *that* mistake again."

Annalee shrugged her shoulders. "Maybe. I suppose."

We were getting to the end of the game, to the last twelve tiles in front of Trish's rack. Suddenly, the ladies were playing very slowly.

Lily was only one tile away from winning a 13579 hand using One Bams, Three Bams, Three Craks, and Five Craks. "I only see two Four Bams," said Lily. "Darnit." She threw out one of her Five Crak tiles.

"Wait, what are you doing?" I asked.

"You're not allowed to throw out a tile on the last wall unless you can account for the other three in the discards," she said. The others nodded their heads.

"That's not an actual rule," I said. "And I can see how it's slowing you down. Hold on." I picked up the Five Crak and put it back on her rack. "Throw the Four Bam."

She did, and—surprise—no one called it. Annalee picked up the next tile and looked at me, relieved. "It's also a Four Bam."

"Do you need it?" I asked her. She shook her head. "Then throw it!"

Trish picked up the next tile from the wall, a Flower. She started to count among the discards.

"I don't see any of these discarded," she said to me. "What should I do?"

"Let's think about this," I said. "How close are you to winning? There are only about two picks left for each of you. If you aren't that close to winning, then definitely look at the exposures and discards and try to throw something safe…

but if I were only one tile away, I wouldn't break up my hand."

Trish looked at her tiles. "Okay. South." It was a good choice because no one else was interested in the Winds: fourteen of the sixteen had already been discarded.

Madeleine, who was waiting on a Nine Dot and a Nine Crak, also picked up a Flower. "I don't see any of these discarded, either," she said.

"How close are you to winning?"

"I only need two tiles," she said.

"Do you feel lucky?" I asked.

"Not really." She discarded one of the Nine Dots.

Lily, still only one tile away, picked a Joker for mah jongg. "I made it!" she said. She laid out her hand for the others to see, and they applauded.

"Okay, don't throw your tiles in yet," I said. "I have a few questions. First of all—do you always play that you can't throw certain tiles on the last wall?"

They nodded.

"Do you have a lot of wall games?" I asked. They agreed that they were pretty frequent. "If Lily had kept the Four Bam and thrown away one of her Five Craks, she never would have won. Correct?" Again, they agreed.

"In a tournament, no one is telling you what you can and can't throw. There's no 'hot' wall, there's no 'cold' wall. There are no such restrictions at any point in the game. The one big penalty is if you throw someone's mahj tile. It's worse if the player has two or more exposures. It won't hurt the other two players, but *you* need to pay attention to what's been exposed because it can cost you points."

They nodded, listening closely. "No 'cold' wall? So, I could call for an exposure on the last wall even if it's not for mah jongg?" asked Annalee.

"Absolutely. That's probably part of why you don't win as much…you haven't been able to complete your hand."

"Let's try another game," said Madeleine. "Do you have any other comments before we start?"

"You shouldn't be talking about what you're playing during the Charleston. Just pass tiles, don't ask for things. You already know that the mush is illegal, and that once you throw something, you can't take it back. Knowing all that, let's try again. Remember that the last wall is as open as the rest of the tiles. The next East is Madeleine."

————

By the end of the morning, the ladies had become more comfortable with playing by tournament rules. The one thing that I still needed to point out was that tournaments required the game be played at a quicker pace, since there was a time limit.

"I have some ideas that can help you speed up your game: don't chat as much during the Charleston, plan ahead to figure out what you will want to throw, and also—no post-mortems."

"What do you mean?" asked Madeleine.

"When the game is over, don't ask, 'Who had my Three Dots?' Don't show everyone the hand you were playing. Just throw in the tiles and start mixing for the next game."

They nodded. "I'm not saying that you can't still do this in your regular game, but in a tournament, there is a time clock. If you don't finish each round on time, then you miss out on a chance to get more points."

I started to explain scoring to them. "I already mentioned that there's a penalty for throwing a player's mahj tile, but it's not as bad as in a real game. You don't have to 'pay double.' The other two players don't lose any points at all." I told them about the ten-point bonuses for picking your own mahj tile and for being Jokerless. "And each player gets ten points if you have a wall game."

"That's a relief," said Annalee. "I'll need to get some points to make up for all the penalties!" They all laughed.

"Oh, there's one other thing. I noticed that no one was paying attention to whether or not Trish's hand was dead, in that other game." I brought up the situation where it was obvious from her exposures—three Three Craks and three Four Craks--that Trish had been trying for the first Consecutive Run hand. She needed a pair of One Craks, but three of them had already been discarded on the table. There was no way she was going to win that hand, since the pair was no longer available.

"I know you're playing a friendly game, and no one wants to hurt anyone's feelings, but even in a friendly game you shouldn't worry about calling a hand dead. It's not personal, it's a fact that she can't win. If you let her keep playing, you're limiting yourself and getting fewer picks. Don't be surprised, in a tournament, if someone calls your hand dead. They want to improve their own chances.

"On the other hand," I continued, "make sure you're right before you call a hand dead. Sometimes there's more than one hand that has the same exposures. If you call a hand dead and you're wrong about it, you'll be called dead yourself."

I realized that I'd just backed myself into a corner with that one. Now they'd be even more reluctant to call another player's hand dead. I mentally shrugged, realizing that they'd probably be playing with more aggressive opponents who *would* know what to do if an opponent's hand was dead. I was just trying to steel them for playing with strangers. At least now they'd know not to burst into tears if someone called their hand dead.

"Do you want to try again in a week or two? Maybe ask another regular group, and the eight of you could mix it up and practice a little more," I suggested.

Lily liked that idea, and I got the others to agree as well.

I wanted to encourage them to join us. "There are going to be a lot of people at that tournament, and there's no reason why the winner can't be one of you!"

My private student, Sherry, was catching on to the basics of the game. She still had yet to compete in a real foursome, though, and I asked her why she wasn't going to the drop-in sessions in the card room.

"I don't feel comfortable there," she said.

"I'm sorry to hear that," I said. "Have you gone to other Clubhouse events?"

"Of course!" she said. "Marty and I went to a lot of activities when we were dating. It was awkward, though. Some of the women were cold to me."

"I think I know why," I said. "People were gossiping that you might have been partially responsible for Marty breaking up with my mom."

She cocked her head at me, obviously puzzled. "Marty didn't…he said that things with Fran ended peacefully, that there were no hard feelings."

I nodded. "Not between him and Mom, but these ladies get pretty gossipy. You should realize that it's high school all over again. If there are two people dating, and they break up and one of them begins dating again, it's assumed that someone was wronged. They start taking sides…"

Sherry laughed. "Absolutely like high school. They thought that I stole Marty? No wonder."

"It never even occurred to you before?" I asked.

She shrugged her shoulders. "I can't figure out the rules here, it's such a small community but it just gets too complicated for me. Even with people I've known for years. There's one woman, in fact she introduced me to Marty. When we were dating, she was one of the *only* people who was being kind to me."

"Well, of course," I said. "She must have been happy to see you together!"

"Oh, sure. She even wanted me to start getting more involved at the Clubhouse. She told me she was going to introduce me to all her friends.

"When I told her we'd stopped dating, she cut me off," she continued. "That's why I can't go to the Clubhouse any more. Now *she's* telling people all sorts of awful things about me."

"Yep. High school. Does she have some kind of connection to Marty?" I asked.

Sherry considered the question. "Not that I know of," she said. "Not that she ever mentioned. I mean, she knew *me* first."

"I'm so sorry. Who is she?"

"Lois Benson," she said.

"Lois Benson set you up with Marty? Really?" I wondered about the timing. "Was this before or after he'd stopped seeing my mother?"

"I don't know, but believe me, none of it was my idea. She thought we'd get along great!"

"And now that you're not with Marty, she's bad-mouthing you at the Clubhouse?"

"All over the Pines, actually," said Sherry. "People I've never seen in my life are giving me dirty looks. No one will play tennis with me, they look the other way when I walk into the Fitness Center. But especially in the card room—I don't feel welcome at Monday Morning Mahj. She had promised she'd teach me how to play mah jongg, and I got all excited—then, *bam!* She cut me off. That's part of why I was so upset, and why I called you."

"So you *were* upset when you left that message. I was worried about you. Then you seemed fine when we met face to face, so I figured it was just allergies!" I admitted.

"You're so sweet," she said. "I appreciate how you're taking me under your wing."

"Wait, let me just piece this together again. You and Lois were old friends..."

"More like acquaintances. I don't know that we were ever friends. We just knew each other for a very long time," she explained.

"Okay. So long-time acquaintance Lois Benson introduced you to Marty Wolf, and as the two of you started dating, she was nicer to you and offered to teach you mahj, and to introduce you around the Clubhouse. When you two broke up, she started talking dirt about you."

"Exactly," said Sherry. "I think that's how it happened. I don't know how I did anything to offend her, other than stop seeing Marty!"

"Strange," I said. I was thinking to myself, *I understand Lois introducing Sherry to Marty to get back at my mom, but if they broke up, why was Lois so hostile? Does she have some special loyalty to Marty?*

"Sherry, you've probably heard the proverb: 'The enemy of my enemy is my friend.'"

"Whoa, wait a second, nobody's an *enemy*, for heaven's sake," she said.

"Even so...it's high school, right? You're on the 'outs' with Lois, and I happen to know some other ladies at the Pines who are equally cut off from her. I swear, they're really very nice people. Maybe you could find some common ground."

Sherry seemed interested. "If you want to make some introductions, I'd be happy to meet them."

On my way to my car, I called my mom. "We need to have an emergency meeting of the Tournament Committee. Tell Carol we're starting a special project."

CHAPTER 24

From our time on the committee, I had seen that Carol and my mom, BFFs, worked well together on strategy. Now I was going to use that friendship to help *my* new friend. I sat in my mother's kitchen with the two of them, sipping coffee, and asked them if they would do me a huge favor.

"You've been here long enough to know how these rumors live and die," I said. "Sherry Kandel is really a sweet person, but she's got an image problem. She's being treated terribly by some of the ladies here. It's not only because of your breakup with Marty. Some of it is from Lois Benson causing trouble. I don't know what you can do to change that…but at least if you're kind to Sherry in public, it will be a start. Please?"

I explained that Sherry and Marty were no longer an item, and that he'd moved on to yet another lady. Neither of them looked very surprised.

"You know," Carol said, "he could have been on the cover of *Smart Women, Foolish Choices.*"

"Are you ever going to let that go?" Mom asked her. "Honestly. There aren't a lot of options out there."

"I'll shut up now," Carol said, grinning.

I mentioned the next big social event: the Fall Formal, Parnassus Pines' answer to a Homecoming dance. "Let Sherry sit with you at your table, be friendly, and maybe introduce her to a few key people. Everyone has the wrong idea about her."

My mother was not generally a vindictive person. I was sure she hadn't contributed to the rumors in the least—

especially since she knew that Sherry had nothing to do with her breaking up with Marty—but she hadn't done anything to squelch those rumors either. Now she could be constructive, and take some positive steps to help Sherry's image.

Carol jumped at the chance. "This could be a lot of fun!"

Mom agreed. "And if Marty's got a new girlfriend, it will be even better!"

———

As it was reported to me, the party went very well.

"First," Mom told me, "I called and asked Elise Wasserman, the Social Committee member in charge of the seating arrangements, to put Sherry at the same table with me and Carol." That little piece of news made it around the Clubhouse circuit quickly, giving people time to consider it even before they could visualize all of them together.

Sherry phoned my mom in advance, and they arranged to arrive at the Fall Formal at the same time. When they walked in together on Saturday night—Carol, Sherry, and Mom—no one said boo. People gave cordial greetings to all three of them.

Carol murmured, "They're being friendly to your face, at least. Now we're going to take it to the next level." She'd taken Sherry's arm and steered her around the room. "Keep up with us, Fran."

Carol first approached Donna Stanton, one of the biggest gossips in the whole development; she was also a grandmother eight times over. "Donna, this is Sherry Kandel. She lives over on Troy Terrace. She's been looking for the best place to buy a baby gift for her grandniece. I just knew you'd have some ideas."

Donna lit up. She started describing some of the boutiques in the surrounding area, and then talked about the customized gift wrap and superior service at her favorite one. "Of course, for ongoing gifts, you'll probably do better just sending a Babies 'R' Us gift card. But for the first present, it's got to be something special." Sherry nodded the whole time, unable to get a word in, and by the end of the lecture, Donna had definitely warmed up to her.

"You're such an expert," said Sherry, smiling. "I really appreciate your advice."

"Any time, dear. Happy to help," said Donna, turning to rejoin her friends. "Enjoy the new baby."

"Next stop, Marge," said Carol. "You take her over there, Fran. Let people see just the two of you together."

Marge Strompf was one of the more athletic Pines residents. She still played tennis or golf at least three times a week. Sherry was a good tennis player, but just as with mah jongg, she'd been forced to resort to private lessons since no one would let her into their group. Unfortunately, that had backfired in the worst possible way: there was innuendo about her and Scotty Morgan, an aging local tennis pro.

My mom wasn't much of an athlete, but she knew just how to pitch to Marge. "Sherry has been working on her net game with Scotty, and he thinks she's going to be a real contender on a doubles team. Do you know of anyone who's looking for a new partner?"

Marge thought for a moment. "How's your serve?"

They talked for a few minutes, and Marge said, "We'll be getting together tomorrow at 10. Why don't you join us?"

Sherry beamed as they walked away. "I'd better be on my A game for her," she said. "She seems like a real killer."

"Are you up for it?" asked Mom.

"Absolutely!"

They found their way to their table. Carol was already there, and when they told her about the tennis victory, she was pleased. "This is how it all starts," she said. "A few words to the right people, and the ice is finally broken."

They saw Marty across the room, dancing with his newest girlfriend, Jeannine.

"This is the easiest part of all," said my mom.

"Hold on," said Sherry. "It's my turn to lead! But please join me."

When the song ended, Marty and Jeannine moved to the edge of the dance floor. Sherry and Mom were waiting for them. There was a momentary hesitation—Marty looked sheepish and Jeannine looked confused.

"Hi, Marty," said Sherry. "So nice to see you again. I don't think we've met," she said to Jeannine. "My name's Sherry Kandel and this is Fran Klein." She held out her hand.

My mother nodded her head. "Welcome to the Pines," she said enthusiastically. "We hope you'll be happy here."

Jeannine was still puzzled and looked back at Marty. She decided to take the ladies at face value. "Thank you," she said. "It's a lovely neighborhood."

She and Sherry began chatting about the landscaping and Jeannine's home town as they walked away from the dance floor toward the ladies' room. My mother steered Marty in the opposite direction, toward the windows where it was quieter, and said, "You know, there's an easier way to do these transitions. You have no idea what havoc you wreak when you bounce from person to person like that."

Again, embarrassed, he looked back at her. "Jeannine says no one would say a word to her once she started dating me. Am I some kind of pariah?"

"Let's just say that you've got a reputation as a serial dater, but somehow the women get the worst of it, socially. We're trying to rescue Sherry's image, and in order to do that, we have to include Jeannine in the bargain. We would appreciate it," she added, "if you could stick with her at least through Christmas. We're not equipped to handle more than two ex-girlfriends at a time."

Marty stood, shocked at her pointed advice. "Yikes. I promise, I'll be good."

"That's all I'm asking, Marty. Try not to mess up anyone else's reputation."

CHAPTER 25

The Monday after the Fall Formal, I invited Carol and my mom over to my house to join Sherry and me for a few hours of mah jongg. The one-on-one lessons had taken Sherry to a place where she was hesitant, but starting to show progress. I knew that it was important for her to experience some real games.

It turned out that we spent more time talking than playing. The main topic, of course, was Operation Reputation Rehab. The three of them told me about the Fall Formal and its aftermath. All in all, they were very pleased with their success.

After the initial audition on Sunday, Marge Strompf had invited Sherry to be her doubles partner—on a trial basis—while her usual partner, Evelyn, was recovering from gall bladder surgery. And when Sherry saw Donna Stanton in the grocery store, Donna stopped to chat for about five minutes.

"I can't thank you ladies enough," Sherry said. "It's nice to have people be friendlier. Even people I don't know are starting to say hello to me."

"It's a combination of people realizing that you're genuinely a nice person, and that you're not with Marty any more," said Carol. "Talk about getting a bad reputation."

"I don't know," said my mom. "No one was saying bad things about me when I was with him."

"Weren't they?" asked Carol. She winked at me. "You wouldn't even tell your own daughter!"

Mom blushed. "I knew it wasn't serious."

"Even so," I said, "it's a relief for me to know that both you and Sherry have moved on to better things...well, away from...I'm just relieved," I said awkwardly.

The four of us managed to complete six games, amid all the gossiping. I left Sherry to figure things out for herself, and I'm proud to say that she held her own against three veteran players. There was one wall game, and Sherry managed to pick her own winning tile on a simple pung-and-kong hand. We were both thrilled.

———

Unfortunately, there wasn't much that Mom or Carol could do about Sherry's problem with Lois Benson. As the tournament plans became more public, Lois had figured out who Carol was, and now both Mom and Carol were on Lois's blacklist. Neither was welcome at the Clubhouse mah jongg game, at least when Lois was there—and she was there *every single time*. The Pines tournament was just a semiannual event. I taught the newbies for a month or two, but then I set them free in the world. Lois still ran the roost—the ongoing card room drop-in games were her only source of power, but they were a big social deal at the Pines. We needed to figure out how to get Sherry into that room without her being attacked by Lois.

When Sherry stuck around my house after Carol and Mom left, to help put away the tiles, I decided to bring up the issue again. "There's obviously something that Lois is holding against you that has something to do with Marty," I said. "She liked you when you were with him, and now she doesn't. Why was she so gung-ho on the match? Are they cousins or something?"

"I don't know, I don't think so. She definitely encouraged it. I know she told Marty all about me before we met."

"Strange," I said. "It doesn't make sense. Maybe there's something else."

Sherry sighed. "I've known Lois a long time. I've known her husband, Jerry, even longer."

"Aha!" I said. "That's the piece I was missing. Say no more."

"Don't be silly. It's not like that," she said. "Jerry was my husband's best friend when they were kids. I think Lois is probably worried that now that I'm a widow, Jerry will leave her for me."

I thought back to how Carol got her condo for such a good price and the story of Charlie and Eddie's widow. "It wouldn't be the first time that happened around here."

"But I never was interested in him that way," Sherry protested.

"Yes, but was he interested in you? And how long ago are we talking about?"

Sherry sighed. "Do you want to hear a story?"

"I always want to hear a story, especially if it's good," I said. I filled up my water bottle and moved over to the couch. "Go ahead."

One hot Sunday afternoon in August 1965, Sherry and her friend Peaches went to the Bronx Beach and Pool Club, a swimming and social establishment for local families. The teens and young adults had their own special area, and Peaches announced that they should set up their towels close to the boys' locker room, so they could see (and be seen by) all the young men.

Peaches was tall and not very curvaceous, but she had an assertive personality. She was smart enough to know that Sherry was the perfect bait. Boys always noticed Sherry, and once they came over, Peaches was able to convince them to stick around. As usual, it worked—a trio of seniors from City College were on their way to the pool when they somehow decided that they'd much rather stay right there in the sun, talking to the girls.

Sherry was generally quiet, and on this particular day had almost nothing to say. Of course, this intrigued the boys that much more. The tallest and most muscular one, Jerry, kept trying to ask her out. "Jerry and Sherry—we ought to go out sometime, huh? That would be funny."

He was flanked by short, round, always-laughing Davey, and Harvey, a skinny boy with glasses and a kind face. Harvey kept trying to get a word in, but it was hard—between Peaches chatting to each of the boys, Davey exploding with laughter, and Jerry focusing all his attention on Sherry, there wasn't much for him to contribute.

Davey said, "We should get together tonight. Harvey's got a car!"

Peaches was all for it. They arranged to meet up and go driving, maybe to a restaurant that the boys knew about, up in Yonkers.

"They've got great pie!" said Davey. Harvey took down Sherry's address and they said their goodbyes.

Once the boys left, Peaches made it clear that she wasn't interested in Harvey. "You can have him. Davey's got the personality and Jerry's got the looks…we'll see who sits in the back with me."

The boys picked them up at Sherry's apartment house. As it turned out, Davey ended up in the backseat with Peaches. Sherry was sandwiched on the front bench between quiet, responsible Harvey and loquacious Jerry, who continued to monopolize the conversation.

"We don't usually get to this part of the Bronx. When we were kids, we always stuck to our own neighborhood. We had a little gang, Harvey and Davey and me and a couple of other guys from Morris Avenue. Just off Grand Concourse. One day, some guys from Highbridge came by, looking for trouble."

Harvey said, under his breath, "They asked if we wanted to buy some magazine subscriptions. They were twelve years old."

Jerry continued his story, completely unaware of Harvey's comments. "One of the guys broke a bottle and challenged me to a fight."

"The kid had a Coke bottle with him, and he accidentally dropped it," said Harvey.

"I kicked it out of his hand and wrestled him to the ground. The other guys were so scared, they ran away," Jerry continued.

"It was dinnertime, and they had to leave. There wasn't any fight," Harvey intoned.

"You can bet those guys never came back to our block again!" said Jerry.

Jerry continued with stories about rescuing a cat who was stuck in a tree, making the all-Borough basketball team in tenth grade, and somebody trying to hold him up at the movie theatre—when he stood up and showed his full size and strength, the guy "ran away like a scared rat."

Under his breath, Harvey continued to provide witty comments about what actually had happened. It was like a confidential play-by-play, subtle but very amusing. As he did this, Harvey kept his eyes on the road and no one heard him but Sherry.

When they reached the restaurant, the pairing continued—Peaches and Davey on one side of the booth, Sherry opposite them with the other two boys on either side of her. While Jerry was sharing a story across the table, Sherry had a moment to speak quietly, directly to Harvey.

"Does he know you talk this way about him?" she asked.

"Not a chance," said Harvey.

He carried on his little commentary while the other three were as loud as ever.

This quintet went on for the rest of the summer, until college began again for the boys. Peaches and Davey ended up breaking up, and the other boys got caught up in schoolwork. One Sunday afternoon in late October, Harvey and Jerry brought flowers to Sherry's apartment and asked if she would come out with them again.

She broke away from her story to explain to me: "I know your generation has a different definition of a 'threesome,' but really, we were pretty innocent. Jerry didn't make any headway with me, having Harvey there the whole time; I felt safe because neither boy would make a move with the other right there; and Harvey could tell that, in my quiet way, I was listening to every word he said."

After two more Sundays like this, Harvey had reached the end of his rope with Jerry and his boasting.

"It's time to make a choice," he said quietly. Still outwardly noncommittal, Sherry watched as Harvey challenged Jerry to their version of a duel:

"I'll play you one-on-one. First person to 11 gets the fair maiden."

This was, of course, ludicrous. Jerry practiced basketball fifteen hours a week for his fraternity team. There was no way in the world that a bespectacled Biology major was going to beat him at his own game.

They went down to the playground and started the match. It was cold and windy, with very few people out on the street. No one was around to referee, and it was up to Sherry to keep score.

Almost instantaneously, Jerry jumped out in front. He was up, 7 points to 0, when Harvey finally got one basket off of him. Rather than being a magnanimous winner, Jerry became irate—he'd wanted to dominate the entire match. Now he decided to punish Harvey for having the audacity to challenge him at his best sport.

Harvey got shoved out of the way for a loose ball and shouted, "Hey!" but Jerry kept playing. He made a beautiful shot, right over Harvey's head, to go up 8-1.

Two simple shots later, Harvey stood on the verge of losing the game and the girl. He came in close, trying to score one more point off of Jerry before the inevitable loss—and Jerry clocked him right in the face with his elbow.

Blood started spurting out of Harvey's nose. His glasses were broken—fortunately, they'd flown off his face, and none of the glass shards got anywhere near him—but he was in absolutely no condition to drive. Jerry realized what he'd done, and spent the entire drive to the emergency room, apologizing, while Sherry held Harvey's head on her lap, in the back seat, trying to keep the blood from spurting everywhere.

Five hours later, she came home, covered in blood. Sherry had ruined her new fake-cashmere cardigan, and her plaid jacket was never the same. Her mother was scandalized that Sherry had been a witness to such violence: "Those boys must be thugs," she fretted. "What will the neighbors think?"

Of course, Jerry was embarrassed to have been so brutal. He had made a terrible mistake. While he won the battle, he lost the war—two weeks later, Harvey proposed to Sherry and she accepted.

Harvey and Sherry were rock solid from there. They had a quick wedding in the spring of 1966, between Harvey's graduating City College and starting medical school at Downstate.

Jerry took out plenty of other girls, but none of them lasted long. Four years later, when Harvey already had started his podiatry training and he and Sherry had bought their first little house in New Jersey, Jerry came out from the City with his new girlfriend, Lois. He introduced them as his best friend and his best friend's wife, but from the beginning, Lois was uncomfortable. She somehow knew that Jerry had been "sweet on" Sherry once, and always saw her as a threat.

———

"To this day," Sherry said, "she still grabs his arm whenever I'm around. If I'd wanted him, I could have had him fifty years ago! Silly woman."

"So she says horrible things about you so that no one else will invite you to play mah jongg?" I asked. That *really* sounded petty.

"Nothing that I've heard directly, but you should see the looks I get. After I stopped seeing Marty, they began treating me like I'm some tramp. You're right, it's exactly like we're all back in high school."

I told her I hadn't had much to do with Lois or her gang. "Lois has a lot of power at the Pines, but there are people who won't let her opinion sway them. I promise you that there are plenty of friendly folks who aren't going to close you out the way she has. Stick with my mom and Carol, you'll be fine."

Sherry nodded her head. "All I can do is hope for the best. I feel sad for Lois," she added. "It must have been hard for her, worrying about her husband straying for all these years."

"I'm sure you never gave her any reason to worry. I doubt he ever did, either."

"I certainly wasn't looking at Jerry. I never gave him a second thought."

We picked up the tiles and I congratulated her again on her earlier win. "You're going to get the hang of this, and you're going to make friends. Things will all work out. I'm sure of it."

"It's the kind of movie that will be on Sundance or IFC. It'll never make it out to theaters near us," I argued.

Roger and I were looking over the listings on Fandango. Lately we'd explored a lot of action/superhero options, and I was tired of them. Finally, we were true empty-nesters and had a lot more flexibility. We could decide on the spur of the moment to go to dinner and a movie—even an art film in Manhattan—and I wanted to take full advantage.

"Number one, it's a bye week for the Giants. Number two, Bill Murray's in it and you love him. Number three, we'll get something interesting for dinner afterward." I thought I made a very compelling case.

"Okay, you win," he said. "Let's get going."

I was happy to begin our adventure. This time we took the Lincoln Tunnel, and caught the movie on the East Side. It ended at around 6:30 p.m., just as the sky was darkening.

"You know what? We're right by Jodi's place. I'm going to see if she wants to come with us for dinner!" I said.

"You didn't call first," he said. "You should at least see if she's home."

"Ah, what the heck, let's just go over. We're only three blocks away!" I insisted.

We showed up in her lobby and the security guard, Sebastian, seemed surprised to see me. He'd never met Roger, of course, but recognized me from several visits to Jodi's apartment.

"Hello, Mrs...?"

"Welt, I'm a friend of Jodi Albert's."

"Of course. I don't think she's expecting you...?" he said, with a questioning tone.

"Do you know if she's in?" I asked.

"I haven't seen her at all today, but I only came on shift at noon. Hmm. Just a moment, please. I will see if she's home." He picked up the house phone.

He mumbled some words into the phone. I heard his re-action. "Yes. Yes, I know. No, they are here in the lobby. Okay. Yes, thank you."

He hung up the phone and turned to me. "She said that you can come up in ten minutes. Please have a seat." He ges-tured at the couches in the well-decorated lobby.

I looked at Roger. "Let's go sit," I said.

"Do you think she's jumping into the shower, or kicking some guy out of the apartment through the back door? May-be she's hiding the remnants of some big junk food binge. Maybe all three?" asked Roger. "And hiding all the liquor bottles, to boot?"

It had become a game for Roger, speculating on the mys-terious life that Jodi led. I'd mentioned to him that I had never seen her in the evening, save for that one time at Ben-jy's graduation/going-away party. When I'd asked her about the migraines, she said she had a doctor and everything was under control.

"Maybe she's the opposite of a vampire," he said. "When it's dark out, she can't function. I'd say she was a werewolf, but we're nowhere near a full moon!"

"Honey, enough. I mean, if you have to tell jokes, let's get them out of the way before we see her. I have no idea whether she's got a sense of humor about this. Maybe she doesn't even think it's weird, and we'll upset her if we make a big deal out of it."

We heard a buzz, and then Sebastian walked over to us. "You may go up now."

"Thank you," I said. We got in the elevator and I pressed the button for the sixteenth floor.

Jodi was waiting at her front door as we got off the elevator, in decidedly unglamorous clothes: sweatpants and a Northwestern hoodie. Her hair was in full frizz, as bad as I'd ever seen it. "Hey. On a Sunday evening, yet. Welcome."

We went into the apartment. Roger looked around, nervously expecting some sort of strange thing to pop out at him. He was casing the place like a tightly wound detective: were there remnants of a drug binge? A dead body in the corner, perhaps?

Jodi merely looked exhausted. "So, what are you guys doing in the City?"

"We went to see a movie. It was pretty good. Are you hungry? Want to come out to dinner?"

"Nah. No, I don't think so." She sat down on the couch. "Do you want a drink, or some crackers or anything?"

"I'm fine," said Roger.

"Were you outside today?" I asked. "The weather was pretty nice."

"I don't usually go out much on the weekends," she said. Now that I considered it, that was also true. Except for the time that I saw her at Citi Field, we met up on weekdays, mid-morning to mid-afternoon.

"So...okay. I didn't mean to interrupt anything," I said.

"It's fine," she said. She seemed much more lethargic than usual. "I'm not up for much, I'm sorry. I just didn't want you sitting around the lobby all night, waiting. That's no good."

I agreed. "Can we bring something back for you? We're thinking maybe Texas barbecue, or this Malaysian fish place, or maybe Ethiopian—no, that doesn't travel well, never mind."

"Honestly, I'm not that hungry. It's nice to see you, though. We're still on for Tuesday, right?"

"Sure," I said. "No big deal. Do you want to go someplace, maybe down the Shore if it's nice? It won't be crowded."

"Let me talk to you on Tuesday morning. I don't know right now." She was trying to hide a grimace. It was clear that she was very uncomfortable and not interested in chatting.

"Okay. There's nothing I can do for you? You're sure?" I asked. Roger and I looked at each other. It was obvious that she looked as bad as she had at Benjy's party. "Are you having another migraine?"

"Not exactly. Don't worry about it." She got up and walked toward the door, indicating that we should go. "I'll talk to you on Tuesday. Sorry I'm not much company."

"It's fine, call me when you can," I said. "Thanks for letting us stop by."

"Yeah," she said, dismissively. "Goodnight."

She shut the door behind us, and I held my hand up to Roger—a signal not to speak until we were safely in the elevator.

"Okay," he said, when the indicator light showed us down at the tenth floor, descending. "I didn't see a guy, I didn't see a needle, I didn't see a bottle of anything...but what the heck?"

"Maybe she went out last night, she had a hangover or something."

"Eighteen hours later?" he asked.

"I don't know. She doesn't drink much at all, with me. I don't think it's a hangover. Maybe it's more migraines. It was kind of rude of us to come by, anyway, without an invitation."

"She didn't seem mad," he said.

"She just didn't seem...like herself," I mused. "Then again, what do we really know about her?" I asked. "I don't usually see her unless it's planned. Daytime, during the week. Maybe there's a whole extra part of Jodi that I *don't* know."

CHAPTER 27

"Come on, you can do this," I said to Jodi. "Just think for a minute. What did you see when you got off the escalator?" I was trying to help her retrace her steps. It was two p.m. on Tuesday, only two days after my "drop-in" visit to her apartment, and we were looking for her car in the lot at the Palisades Center Mall. She had completely forgotten where she'd parked.

She had asked me to meet her there because she'd been scouting locations for Sam's eleventh birthday party. Both Peter and Nancy worked long hours at their ophthalmology practice, and since Jodi was currently a woman of leisure, she was put in charge of planning the event. The venue had to be well-supervised, big enough for twenty-five boys, and within an hour of home. Jodi had fudged a little on the distance, but figured there were enough choices at Palisades Center that she'd be able to find just the right place.

Unfortunately, even though we'd found an interesting combination (a movie at the IMAX theater plus climbing on the giant indoor rock wall), she'd forgotten where she parked. "I know I met you near Dave & Buster's, but I went to Modell's first, to look at running shoes. Or was it Sports Authority? Or did I start at Target?"

I tried to approach it systematically, like I would about any other lost item. "Let's think about this again. Do you remember whether you parked in the garage or outside?" I asked.

She furrowed her brow. "It must have been the garage, because I didn't bring my umbrella, I just took an escalator upstairs."

So we knew it was somewhere in that cavernous garage. "All right, what do you remember seeing at the top of the escalator?" I was trying to figure out whether she'd used the East or West entrance. The mall was so big that the two sides could have had their own zip codes.

Patiently, methodically, I talked Jodi through the morning's events. She seemed sure that she had parked somewhere underground, but rather than wander aimlessly, we went to my car together. We'd be able to survey the region much more quickly that way.

Jodi was frustrated and embarrassed, and near tears: the mall and the garage were absolutely immense, and she felt like she would never find her car. It was cold and raining, but at least we were safe and dry once we got to my Camry. I put on the headlights and proceeded slowly down the garage ramp. I wove up one aisle and down the next, as she pressed the button on her car's electronic remote, hoping for a response. So far, no luck. Cars in front of us were searching for empty spots; we were looking at every single car that was already parked.

Finally, in the West garage, between two large SUVs, we found her little silver Acura. I parked in a nearby space as we both caught our breath; it had been a tense fifteen minutes or so.

She wiped her eyes. "Does this happen a lot?" I asked her.

"No, not often. It's a lot easier when I park outside, or when I stick to familiar places. This is the first time I've been here in a long time."

"Oh, I get it, believe me," I said. "This parking lot would drive anyone crazy. I'm sure it was the inspiration for that episode of *Seinfeld*—you know, the one where they can't find Kramer's car and Jerry gets arrested for public urination?"

She'd stopped crying. "That was pretty bad. I'm fine when I do routine stuff, but this mall really threw me off. I'm worn out from the noise, and from going to one party place after another."

I nodded, concerned. "Are you getting enough sleep? Is it the change in weather?"

She exhaled. "No. No, I'd better tell you. I've been avoiding it, but you need to know what's going on with me."

I wasn't sure what she was about to tell me. Maybe it would explain all the odd behavior. Was it more than migraines? Was she experiencing early-onset Alzheimer's? A bad reaction to medication? I waited, and tried to look as nonjudgmental and supportive as possible.

"I've got some neurological issues. I get tired easily, and sometimes I have pretty bad brain fog. They thought it might be Lyme disease, but it's more likely that I have Chronic Fatigue Syndrome," she said. "I have a team of doctors and I see a therapist every week."

"Is that what you're doing, why you're so busy in the evenings?" I asked.

"Oh, no way. I see them all during midday. I'm usually wiped out by sundown. On bad days I'll crawl into bed by 4 p.m."

Suddenly I understood a little better: she turned off the phone because she was exhausted and unable to deal with people, not because she was actually busy. "How long have you known about this?" I asked.

"I first realized that something was wrong about four years ago. My first thought was that it might be MS—you know, multiple sclerosis. I mean, I was in my forties, and I was worn out all the time. The fatigue was the impetus for shifting more of my work to Gary," she explained. "It was my doctor's idea and I thought he was pretty smart. The doctor, I mean. At the time I thought Gary was smart, too, but we see that I was way off base about *that*." She smiled ruefully.

The work situation finally made sense. There's blind love, but Jodi was too shrewd of a businesswoman to just blithely hand her business over to her boyfriend. She'd been faced with a serious problem. She was no longer able to handle the workload physically, and Gary must have been (at the time) the obvious choice to take over the company. She probably convinced the Board quickly, without even doing an official search.

"So does your mom know about your situation? Did your dad know?"

She shook her head. "I never wanted to worry Dad. I already knew that he was very sick, and the last thing he needed was my medical problem on top of that. Same with Ma. I didn't want to upset her any further. I found a good team of doctors in the City, separate from anyone I knew out in Jersey. I made Peter my primary contact and I swore him to secrecy."

"So how can I help? What do you need?"

She looked at me gratefully. "The first thing, you're already doing. My therapist says it's important that I keep up a social life, even if on a small basis, and you've been great. Plus I admit it's a relief having someone else know what's going on with me. Obviously, Nancy knows too, but she's wrapped up with work and the kids, and I barely see them. I have day-to-day stuff that I just don't want to bother them about."

I nodded. "Whatever you need—rides to physical therapy, someone to walk with, help with shopping or laundry. Do you know of a good book I can get to read up on this?"

Jodi laughed. "Man, you really *are* 'in.' I just need to sit here a minute more and take a breath. I'm glad we found the car, but I'm not sure that I'm okay to drive home right now, especially in the rain."

"Okay," I said, "that's fair. Should I drive you home? Or is that a bad idea?"

"Bad idea. I know you mean well," she said quickly, "but how the heck would I ever get back here to get my car? Let's remember where we parked this time and go back upstairs. Maybe we can find a covered spot where we can get some fresh air—*not* a smoking area."

As we made our way to the escalator, she looked at me quizzically. "It's funny. You, Peter, Nancy, my doctors…oh, and my pharmacist…are the only ones who know. I was afraid to tell Gary, and now I'm glad I didn't. He probably would have dropped me even sooner."

I shook my head. "You know, I hate that guy, and I never even met him."

"He wasn't the worst guy in the world. We had fun for a while. Seriously, Talia, it kind of makes sense that you know. It's lucky for me that our mothers pushed us together."

CHAPTER 28

My mother had done an excellent job organizing the Pines tournament. She was able to recruit the more open-minded Clubhouse players as well as the private home groups and people who hadn't played in years. She got an overall turnout of 108 people, bright and early on a Sunday morning in the middle of November.

The logistics involved in running this kind of an event are not what you might expect. Sure, you need score sheets, pens, and enough tiles and tables for everyone, but the most important things had nothing to do with the game of mah jongg. No matter what the tournament organizers did, someone would complain. There was a draft on one side of the room and too much sun on the other. It was never the right temperature. Some ladies complained that they were dying of the heat, and others kept asking if anyone had a sweater, because they were freezing.

The refreshments were the most debated topic: Was there coffee out at all times? Why or why not? Should people be allowed to bring coffee to the table? What was the "*and*" in "coffee and"—was it just some stale Entenmann's donut holes, or something homemade? And what was for lunch? Something hot? A deli platter? A buffet or waitress service? Would there be a dessert course?

It was impossible to please everyone. If you went high-end, the women would mutter that waitress service was a waste of money. If you tried to be less extravagant, they would whisper among themselves that the cold buffet was "cheap."

If they weren't complaining outright, the ladies loved to rehash previous incidents. The controversy over allowing beverages in the game room had been sparked by a minor event which had since achieved legendary status. It was a seminal moment in the history of Parnassus Pines. I must have had ten women tell me that one of Lois Benson's tournaments had been ruined—"ruined!"—by someone spilling coffee on the tiles. I could picture maybe one table having to suspend play, faced with sopping tiles and possibly even a damaged scorecard, but the entire tournament was *ruined*?

Mom had a diplomatic way of handling the *kvetching*. After years of dealing with cranky parents at the day school, this was easy. She smiled sweetly; shuffled score sheets, looking very busy; and said to all complainers, "That's an excellent point. I'd love to hear your advice about how to fix it, for next time."

Carol, sitting next to her at the organizer table, was much more direct:

"Rose, the donuts are *fine*. No one came here expecting a gourmet meal."

"Sydelle, if you need a sweater, raise your hand. I'm sure someone will lend you hers."

"I'm sorry, Lenore, I'll ask if anyone brought a spare hearing aid battery with them, but you may have to go home at the lunch break to get one."

All I had to do was keep an eye on the mah jongg games and enforce the time limit. There were specific rules on scoring, and I had to be ready to answer questions from any of the twenty-seven tables, at any time. I stood at the far end of the room, looking out like a sailor on top of a mast, scanning the room in search of a raised hand.

Sure enough, Kitty at Table 21 had a question. "We went through the Charleston and Natalie decided she wanted to stop it after the first left, but no one heard her and we kept going. What do we do?"

At a tournament, the director's word is law. It's a lot like settling arguments between small children, and I wielded great power on a question like this. I asked, "Who kept going? Everyone, or just one of you?"

"Just me and Brenda," Kitty admitted. "I gave her the second left and she picked it up."

Brenda looked miffed. She must have liked the tiles she'd received.

"Did anyone else look at theirs?" I asked.

They shook their heads. Natalie was upset. "I told them to stop."

I pursed my lips and thought for a moment. "None of you heard her?"

"It's noisy in here," Kitty explained. She made an excellent point. It was like a loud restaurant. The tables were packed in tight. Some chairs were only inches away from one another.

"I think we have to give Natalie the benefit of the doubt here," I said. "From here on in, no one goes on to make their second left pass without confirming with all players. I'll make an announcement. Brenda, please return the tiles to Kitty." Brenda scowled at me, and handed three tiles to Kitty. Natalie hadn't looked at Brenda's pass yet, and gave the little tripod right back to her.

I turned on the microphone and announced, as loudly as I could, "Ladies! May I please have your attention? It is VERY NOISY in here." The noise modulated. "Please keep the chatter to a minimum. We just had an issue about stopping the Charleston after the first left—a player said she wanted to stop, but she couldn't be heard. I suggest that you make sure that everyone at the table wants to continue before you make the second left pass. Thank you."

There was murmuring. I could only imagine how, for years to come, there would be talk about how "Fran's daughter interfered with the passing." Brenda might be so upset that she'd stop talking to my mother, and tell anyone who would listen (particularly Lois Benson) that I was a *terrible* tournament director. Of course, it was possible that Brenda would go on to get the highest total score, despite this one blip, and say I'd done a great job. You never could tell with these ladies.

Other minor problems arose. Each round, I had to keep checking that the ladies were in their proper positions. Invariably someone would move to the wrong place, insisting that she belonged there. It really did feel like a preschool birthday party. I was running a game of Musical Chairs, except that I had meticulously designed it so that each person had a seat for every round. There should have been no reason for two people to fight over the same spot.

There was also an aspect of being homework monitor: I had to make sure that the score sheets were properly completed. I had asked everyone to write an "X" instead of a zero for any hand that was scoreless, so that it could not be altered into a ten (or more). Each score sheet also had to be witnessed by another player, as confirmation.

My mother and Carol took care of tallying the score sheets for me, so I was able to give updates during the second game of each round. "Cookie Meyers had the high score for round one, with 125 points," I announced. I asked her to raise her hand. There were oohs and ahhs as I handed Cookie a ten-dollar bill.

Another fun event was announcing the "hand" of each round: the first player to win the specially designated combination would shout "I made it!" and I would trot over to verify. She too would win an extra ten dollars.

Most ladies—I'd say 95 out of 108—were adorable: sweet, enthusiastic, grateful, patient. There were about a dozen professional *kvetchers* who complained nonstop about the heat, the food, the noise, the light. The chairs (the *Clubhouse* chairs! The ones they used for every meeting, party, and event) were suddenly "so uncomfortable." And why were they getting such bad tiles?!

Above them all was "The One." Always, always at a tournament there is "The One." I wouldn't know beforehand who it might be; I had no expectations or prejudices about her. But sure enough, there would be one super-aggressive, hostile player. She'd tell the other women at her table that they didn't know the rules. I'd hear shouting from across the room. "Ah, there she is," I would say to my mom. "Gotta go put out that fire!"

This woman could be a Lucille, an Amanda, a Tina, a Belinda—and, of course, at one point her name was Lois Benson. The name and the face might change, but the behavior was consistent. She thought she knew everything about mah jongg, and dictated to the poor ladies at her table. It was thoroughly unpleasant for everyone. She'd tell them they were stupid: "Why'd you throw that?" She'd tell them they were taking too long. She'd slap their hands if they tried to take an exchanged Joker from the top of her rack. She'd say they didn't belong at a tournament. No one had fun with her. Fortunately, in each of the dozen or so tournaments I've given, I've never had to deal with more than one or two players like that. If I identified someone and told her, "Your behavior is unacceptable, and you won't be welcome at future events unless you can show respect to the other players," she usually became more docile. I had her name on file and would ask other people if they noticed whether she had calmed down. She generally did. I would have hated to have to ban someone—the ultimate "time-out."

The problem was that this kind of egregious behavior floated around the room. It was like the arcade game Whac-A-Mole--if you deterred the creature from coming out by whacking it back into its hole with a mallet, it would come up in another spot.

In the tournament, the bad behavior was the "mole." A seemingly nice, civil player could snap one day and *pow,* we had a new monster on our hands, surprising us as she rose from a different spot in the room. Why did this happen? Maybe she was giving up caffeine, per her doctor's orders. Maybe she had suffered a loss recently and was out of sorts. Maybe she just plain lost patience with the world. A player who had been nice—perhaps a little opinionated and pushy (but aren't we all?)—suddenly could become that day's "Dragon Lady." I hoped today's wouldn't turn out to be Brenda, but I kept an eye on her.

Toward the end of the second round, the noise level rose again. I had already announced that we would be having a ten-minute break, and encouraged the players who had completed round two to leave the game room and hold their conversations in the foyer. Of course, no one felt that they were the cause of the noise, and there were five or six loud conversations going on while the other ladies were trying to finish on time.

I turned on the microphone. "If you have finished your round, *please* go out into the foyer." No one was budging. "This room must be quiet. Thank you."

As a few of the groups meandered out into the hallway, I heard some grumbles and muttering. I knew that if they had still been playing, these ladies would have been the first to complain about the noise level. It's always someone else who's the problem.

"Five more minutes," I announced. It was almost 11 a.m. and we had another round to finish before the lunch break. I looked up and saw that Sherry was standing at the doorway. I held up a finger and gestured for her to wait until the round was complete.

When the last of the second-round groups had handed in their score sheets, I walked over to Sherry, who was still waiting by the door. "Wow, this is so wonderful," she said, smiling. "I have never seen so many people playing together all at the same time!"

"It's not as wonderful as it seems. It gets pretty noisy here, with the tiles mixing and people calling out discards. I don't think you're ready yet, but maybe in a few months."

She agreed and then told me that she had been in the

Clubhouse Fitness Center. "It's so empty today. I guess everyone's with you!"

I nodded. "It will probably be quieter at the Stop & Shop for the next few hours too. Now's your chance to get all the best produce!" She laughed and ducked out of the room.

We still had a third round before lunch. Things went smoothly until the final fifteen minutes. I had been wandering from table to table, checking on how things were going, and for the second time in ten minutes noticed that one of the players at Table 8, Anita, was thoroughly exasperated. She kept rolling her eyes, impatient with her tablemate.

I went over to observe more closely. One of those recent prep students, Madeleine, was in the midst of a decision. I checked the score sheet and saw that the group was still on their third game of the round. Anita pointed at the sheet and at the tiles on the table. Only about half of the tiles had been played. "We're never going to finish on time, at this rate," she grumbled. "We still have another hand after this one."

"Please be patient, Anita, I'm sure Madeleine's just figuring out this one thing," I said. I didn't say it aloud, but thought, *You'd expect the same treatment, wouldn't you?*

Madeleine arranged the tiles one way and then another on her rack, and finally discarded, saying, "Okay. Three Dot."

The next player, Eileen, picked and threw, then Anita, and Tracy, and it was back to Madeleine again. Madeleine picked up the next tile and stared at it.

Anita looked like she wanted to scream.

Madeleine put the tile on her rack, flipped things one way and then another, and announced, "Mah jongg."

Anita really did scream...but, realizing how foolish she looked, stifled herself almost immediately. I smiled to myself as I walked away, reflecting on the karma of mah jongg.

It was the Tuesday following the Parnassus Pines tournament, and Jodi and I were eating lunch at a quiet restaurant in midtown Manhattan.

"Do you remember Hebrew school?" she asked. "Sam was telling me about what it's like now. It sounds a lot better than when we were kids. The cantor's young, and Israeli teenagers come and talk to them. Pretty cool."

"It's not like you were focused back then," I told her. "I remember having to bring two pencils to class, because you *always* forgot."

"I knew you would bring me one," she said. "So you were more reliable than I was. Is that so bad?"

"Nah," I said. "And remember those youth group after-parties, like at Renee Barden's house?"

"Oh, I got so sick that night," she said. "Where did I get a pint of schnapps? I was only fourteen. What was I thinking? Chocolate milk and peppermint schnapps…uch. I won't even eat Thin Mints any more, it put me off chocolate mint forever!" She laughed. "But you were so nice to me."

"That's just how I roll," I said. "I was always on the outside, looking in, but when I saw you so miserable, I had to help."

"You're good people, Talia Klein," she said.

"Talia Klein Welt," I reminded her. "You forget about Roger."

"No one can forget about Roger. What a sweetheart. How did you guys meet, anyway?"

"We were in the same dorm, sophomore year. He was the

only other person in Stratton Hall watching *St. Elsewhere* in the common room—everyone else was out drinking at 10 p.m. on Wednesday nights. Romance blossomed," I added.

"Sophomore year? Wow, that's a really long time ago," she said.

"Sounds like around the time that you met the nice Jewish pre-med," I reminded her.

"Indeed it was."

"Do you know what happened to him? Did you keep in touch?"

She looked embarrassed, as if she'd been caught lying. "He's part of the medical team I've been using. After graduation, I stayed in Chicago and he moved here and went to Columbia Medical School. When I got sick and didn't know what was wrong, I called him first. I trust him."

"Makes sense. You know he's steady and reliable, you just didn't want to marry him. What's his specialty?" I asked.

"He's a neurologist."

"Well, that's convenient. Is he married?" I asked.

"Oh, yeah," she said. "Very. Three kids, lives in Westchester. A dog. A boat. His wife has written two kosher cookbooks."

"Wow," I said. "I guess...well...what can you say to that?" I started laughing. "He deserves a good life, doesn't he? He sounds like he's a decent guy."

"Sure," she said. "And twenty-year-old me was an idiot. No, that's not true. I don't know that it was the wrong decision at the time. Besides, if we'd gotten married right after college, I could not have had the career that I did. You know, it's all timing."

"Absolutely," I agreed.

"So listen," she said, "my schedule got switched around because of Thanksgiving. I have an appointment this afternoon in his office. Do you want to come too?"

"Are you kidding?" I asked. I was dying to meet the neurologist from Westchester. It would give me some insight into Jodi's past.

We spent the rest of lunch talking about the 1980s—the endless hours watching the same fifteen videos, over and over, on MTV; the bad cult movies, the clothes, *Saturday Night Live* sketches. It seemed like only yesterday, yet in another way it seemed like ancient history.

The best part was that even though our colleges had been a thousand miles apart, some of our experiences were almost exactly the same: we were both terrible science students, and our respective boyfriends had helped us through our required courses; we'd both been involved in Student Leadership, me as Class Secretary and her as Social Liaison of the Panhellenic Association; and we'd both had great on-campus jobs in the library.

"It was the best place to be. Everyone in my class would come by the Reserved Reading Room, especially during the 7 to 10 p.m. shift," she said.

I agreed. "The middle of the day was like a graveyard. Nobody came. From what Abby tells me, it's totally different now. All of her college professors just post links online. And they let students *rent* books, can you believe it? Undergrad, anyway."

Jodi said, "That could have saved me hundreds of dollars. Thousands, maybe. What a great idea."

It was her turn to pick up the check, and then we headed downstairs to get my car. Dr. Belkin's office was in the hospital, way uptown in Washington Heights, and I was glad that I was able to drive Jodi instead of making her take a cab.

We approached the medical area and she directed me to the valet parking stand at the Milstein Building. I opened my window and she leaned across, greeting the attendant warmly.

"Andre," she said, "meet my best friend, Talia."

"Hello, Miss Talia. Pleasure to meet you," he said. "Are you going to be here long today, Miss Jodi?"

"I don't think so, probably an hour," she said. "Can I bring you back a coffee? It's crazy cold out!"

"You're very kind. Tall nonfat latte, one pump caramel, please."

"You got it!" she said, as we climbed out.

"I left the keys in the cup holder," I told Andre, trying to keep up with Jodi's whirlwind exit. She seemed to know everyone at the hospital: the security guards, the ladies at the Starbucks counter, two orderlies on their break.

"So you're a frequent flyer here?" I asked.

"I've been coming here for years. Inpatient testing, outpatient monthly visits. I think they want to name one of the ladies' bathrooms after me," she said. "For a mere 750 grand or so."

"Money well spent," I said. "Where are we headed?"

"Neurological Institute. Third floor. It's in a separate wing."

We arrived in the Neurological Institute's suite of offices, and the receptionist seemed somewhat surprised to see Jodi in such good spirits.

"Miss Albert, you're…you seem full of energy today!" she chirped.

"Yes, Nicole, I've brought my friend Talia with me. Is Dr. Belkin sticking to his schedule today?"

"Yes, he finished his rounds earlier than usual. Have a seat, it won't be more than five minutes or so."

We sat in the softly muted, color-coordinated waiting room. There were two other patients in the room. One was an older man, hunched over in the corner; his companion, probably his wife, was speaking quietly to him. The other was a younger woman, maybe thirty-five or so, who was nervously chewing her nails.

"That was what I was like," said Jodi. "I always came by myself. I was terrified, didn't know what they would tell me. I was afraid I had a brain tumor, or maybe multiple sclerosis. Very scared."

"And now?" I asked.

"They're still testing for minor variations, but in the meantime, as Mike says, 'We're addressing the symptoms.' He says it doesn't much matter what it's called, as long as they're treating each of the individual problems."

"Makes sense," I said. "But with all those scans and tests, they're still not sure?"

She shrugged. "If anyone knows what to do, it would be him. He's no dummy."

A younger woman, wearing purple hospital scrubs, said, "Miss Albert? Come on in."

Jodi stood up. "Come meet him, it'll be fun," she said. "It's okay, I don't remove my clothes or anything."

We walked past the reception desk and into Examination

Room 3. Jodi sat on the examination table while I stood, useless, off to the side. The young woman took Jodi's blood pressure and temperature and then left us alone. About two minutes later, there was a knock, and then the door opened. A middle-aged, slightly balding man in a white coat entered the room.

"Hey, Jodi—and…?"

"Talia Welt," I said. "I'm an old friend of Jodi's. Nice to meet you."

"Mike Belkin. I'm an old friend of Jodi's too," he said. "Did she tell you?"

"Yeah, pretty handy having a friend in the business," I said. "She says you take good care of her."

"We're trying. Excuse me." He focused his energy on Jodi. "How are you feeling today?" He took a small flashlight and started examining her eyes.

"Really great," she said. "Talia and I had a lovely day out. Lunch at the Time Warner Center."

"Very nice," he said. "Good to be active." I could see that despite the banter, he was all business, paying close attention to her reactions. "You seem to have a little more energy than last time."

"Being with Talia gives me a boost. Oh, I should tell you, I had some wine a week or two ago…"

"Jodi, what did we say?" he admonished. His tone was too paternal, almost condescending, but clearly he cared.

"Yeah, you were right. It was not a successful evening. At least I stayed in my building."

"Evening. Good. So…you've been seeing Caroline every week?"

"Yes," she said. She turned to me. "My therapist."

"And Ashley?"

"Yep." Again, to me: "My physical therapist."

"Good. And we got back your latest blood work. It doesn't seem like your liver's been affected. I think we'll keep you on the same meds for now."

She shrugged at me. "I guess that's good."

"Listen, Jodi, I'm glad you brought your friend with you. It's important for people to know about your illness. You need support more than just once a week, in an office." His voice showed genuine compassion. I was impressed. Perhaps it was only because they were old friends, but he seemed worried about her overall well-being, not just her medical condition. I tried to picture him thirty years younger. He must have been deeply hurt when she left him.

"I know, I know," she said, trying to push off his concern.

"It's about quality of life," he said. "You shouldn't be alone. There's proof that depression, anxiety—without a good support network, you're just going to have a harder time." He looked up at me. "Do you live nearby?"

"I'm in Jersey, like her mom. Jodi's been talking about moving out there to be closer to us."

"Sounds like an excellent idea," said Dr. Belkin. "I'd say, the sooner the better."

CHAPTER 30

Our pre-Thanksgiving trip to Dr. Belkin's uptown office was clearly one of Jodi's better days; both he and the nurses remarked that she had a lot of energy and looked good.

On the other hand, there were days and even weeks when she felt like she'd been run over by a truck. Nights when she didn't get a moment of sleep, and spent the next day exhausted. Times when her mind and body just shut down. It was unpredictable, and both emotionally and physically difficult. One of my jobs would be to try and help her maximize the good and minimize, or at least learn to cope with, the bad.

The Tuesday after Thanksgiving, Jodi woke up feeling like it might be a good day. She called me and I volunteered to pick her up in the City. She never knew just how tired she was going to get, and we didn't want to have her be stranded somewhere when she couldn't make it home.

"So where are we going?" she asked, practically bouncing into the car.

"I was thinking the beach, maybe? Nowhere too far..." I suggested. We agreed that Long Branch would be a good choice. There was a nice boardwalk there and it wouldn't be an all-day drive.

We spent the trip listening to SiriusXM's *'70s on 7* channel, and as I drove, Jodi amused herself by not looking at the monitor as each song came on. She tried to name the artist and the title of the song. Some were easy: "China Grove" by the Doobie Brothers, "Operator" by Jim Croce, "Free Bird" by Lynyrd Skynyrd. It got a little trickier when they played the one-hit wonders like "The Night Chicago Died" by Paper Lace and "Jackie Blue" by the Ozark Mountain Daredevils. Sometimes we both sang along. The time passed quickly, and we reached Ocean Avenue by noon.

"I can't believe how built up it is!" she exclaimed. There were bright condominium townhouses and high-rises all along Ocean Avenue, facing the shore. The dunes were a mess, and most things like patio furniture, grills, and planters were locked up or chained together. Even though the breeze was strong, we tried to pretend it was still summer.

I cruised down the Avenue, hoping to find some stores, and particularly restaurants, that were open even in the off-season. I'd heard that some people lived there year-round, so I was optimistic that there would be a good place for us to get some lunch. Sure enough, we found a cute little coffee shop—"*not* a Starbucks," Jodi had insisted—and went inside.

It was a cozy place, with another table of slightly older women sitting nearby. One was lamenting how hard it had been to get outside last winter. "I had to take Shasta for her walks, but that was it—some days, I just put down newspaper and said, 'Take it or leave it, we're not going out!'"

Her friends agreed. "I'm not sure how many more years I can take, up here. I thought it would be easier near the Shore, but remember? It broke 40 degrees maybe twice the whole winter."

"My friend in Coral Gables complained because there were a few days when it *dropped* to 40." They all laughed.

Jodi looked at me. "Is that going to be us? Are we going to be able to handle these arctic winters?"

"I don't know," I answered truthfully. "Roger and I are here because of his job, and because Mom's here. Mom's here because Roger and I are here. But where would we go? Florida? Arizona? California?"

"Hawaii sounds good!" said Jodi. "I'm going to get a little house and hire a pool boy, and I'll be all set."

I nodded. "Okay, just make sure there's enough room for all the visitors. And your mom? Is she coming too?"

"I don't think she likes coconuts," she said. "Maybe it's not the right place."

We continued to daydream about warmer climes. "Let's go outside for a little. Maybe the breeze has died down and we can sit on a bench," I told her.

We walked out of the café, went down the block a bit, and found a nice bench facing the ocean where the view wasn't obstructed by sand dunes. We looked out at the gray-green waves and saw a gull desperately searching for food.

After about four minutes, Jodi said, "Yeah. Great concept, but I'm freezing. Let's go back inside."

We came back into the coffee shop, and the owner didn't even glance at us. Apparently it was common to try to deal with the wind and then give up and go back inside.

I took the opportunity to get a little more serious than usual. Jodi and I had a lot of fun recounting stories from our childhood and adolescence, talking about ancient history, but I got the sense that it was a diversion. She was trying to avoid talking about her current circumstances. I still had

Mike Belkin's voice in my head, and his words—"the sooner the better"—were haunting me.

"So listen," I said. "Have you given any more thought into moving out to New Jersey? Maybe put together a local medical team, and let your mom in on your little secret?"

Jodi was acting like Cleopatra—"Queen of Denial." Not talking about her illness with her mother made it somehow less real. In at least this one key relationship, she wanted to keep up the pretense that she was perfectly well, that *she* was the strong one, that she could help her mother. I could see she wasn't ready to break down that image for either of them.

She shook her head, not budging. "Ma's got enough on her plate, settling Dad's estate. She doesn't need to deal with a sick daughter."

"Jodi, what did Mike say? It's important for you to have a support system. You need to let more people into your world." I tried another direction: "Do you ever see your friends from your old life, back when you were working?"

She snorted. "Are you kidding? It was so hard, being a woman with my own business. I didn't have friends, not in any intimate sort of way. That was part of what brought me and Gary so close together. He was one of the only people who wasn't afraid of me, and I was grateful for the companionship. I had a reputation as kind of a bitch," she confessed. "I had to be tough."

I nodded. It hadn't occurred to me that she'd built up walls all those years. I was starting to get a picture of just how lonely her life had been. First, people thought she was a perfectionist, all work, and made of stone. Later, when she showed weakness, they really turned away. I felt sad to think of how hard it must have been for her. Our friendship brought her comfort on more than one level. If she wanted to indulge in slumber party-style confessions and pop culture quizzes every now and then, what was the harm? At least she trusted me with her important secrets.

"You'll tell your mom when you're ready. I get it, but I do think you should start doing more research on moving home. It's time to make more of an effort to find a place to live, and at least a therapist and trainer out here. If you want to stick with going to the City to see Mike, I totally understand, but let's get the transition started. What do you think?"

She nodded. "I'll admit it. I'm ready to be a Jersey girl again."

"Speaking of," I said, "do you want to get a t-shirt before we go? Some kind of proof that you've been down the Shore? A henna tattoo, maybe? A coffee mug?"

"Let's save it for next time," she said.

As we drove back up the Parkway, listening to "Saturday Night" by the Bay City Rollers, Jodi thanked me. "It's been great having a change of scenery. I need to figure out what I want, and where I want to be, but I appreciate that you're in my corner. You're a good friend."

"No problem," I said. "I'm sure you would do the same for me." We were both quiet for a moment, as the song ended. The radio played the Sirius promo spot, and then a new song began.

Is this the real life? Is this just fantasy? "'Bohemian Rhapsody' by Queen!" she shouted.

When I was back teaching at Sherry's house, I looked over her photos again. There were several nice pictures of her husband, but I didn't see any children. I wondered what kind of a life she had led— they had travelled to some interesting places, but here she was, alone.

I let her know I appreciated her work. "You should have been a professional photographer," I said. "Some of these compositions are beautiful, quite impressive. My son would tell you all about the angles and the light, and how well you captured it."

She smiled. "Thank you. I was a professional, once, sort of…I mean, I was hired to be a photographer, but it wasn't artistic or anything."

The story about Jerry and Harvey had been a lot of fun. I figured she must have other great stories to tell. "Was this before or after Jerry socked your husband on the nose?"

She said, "Oh, you remembered that? Actually, it was before that happened. A long time ago." She sounded a little wistful.

"Then you must have been just a kid!"

She agreed. "I was barely eighteen. I had answered an ad to go up to the Concord, one of the big resorts in the Catskills. They had lots of job openings. I didn't have any waitressing experience or typing skills, and I definitely didn't want to do housekeeping.

"They asked if I knew how to work a camera. I was pretty and young, so they asked me to work on the photography staff. You know, taking pictures at the cocktail parties and the dinners. Someone else would do all the processing work, overnight, and after a day or two I was supposed to set up a display and show off the proofs in the lobby. The hotel sold these little plastic photo viewers called scopes, that included a miniature photo, and if a customer liked the picture, we could arrange for enlargements too."

"I went up to the Concord when I was a kid!" I said. "I know exactly what you're talking about. They had those triangle photo viewers with the name of the hotel. That was *you*?!"

"That was me!" she said proudly. "Most of the pictures weren't very artistic, though. I'd get the people at a table to pose together, or a family at a cocktail party. Everyone used to get dressed up in the evening, especially on a Saturday night when they had a big entertainer coming. It was nice. Things were a lot more formal, even in summer—at least at mealtime."

"It sounds like it was kind of routine, though. Did they ever have you take nature photos or sports or anything, or just the people at the parties?" I asked.

"The parties were where they made all the money. Couples dancing, or families together. That sort of thing. Sometimes I went outside during the day and took pictures of activities, but most of the time it was formal shots. But no, it wasn't boring. I met some nice people. And I saw mah jongg," she added. "There probably were people in my neighborhood who played, but I saw it a lot at the Concord, with ladies of leisure who would sit around the card room or the pool, playing for hours. I never thought I'd have the time to learn."

I took the hint. "So here we are," I said. "Today we're going to talk about switching your hand. Remember how last week you were trying for the first Consecutive Runs hand but then someone else put out three One Craks?"

She thought for a moment. "I had almost all the other Crak tiles in my hand. It ruined my plan."

"Let's look at the card. Was there another hand that used those tiles? Look at the fours and fives. Now look further down in the Consecutive Runs section. See the hand that uses two suits with four consecutive numbers: three of a kind and four of a kind in one suit, and then three of a kind and four of a kind in another?

"So the next time that you're trying for that Consecutive Runs hand, maybe keep a few other tiles from the adjacent numbers." I looked through the tiles and put them out on display to illustrate my point. "You see? Three Four Craks, four Five Craks...you could have that be the first part of 4-5-6-7, or the end of 2-3-4-5."

Sherry nodded. "So I should have switched to the Four and Five Craks, plus twos and threes in another suit?"

"Exactly." I smiled at her. "You're going to be a great player, I can see it. The gears are still turning in there."

She smiled. "I told you, I've got a great *teacher*."

"The main thing is, don't have too much of your hand exposed if you don't have the pairs. One exposure won't hurt you, but with some hands, two exposures give you away. If you're unable to complete a hand, you're at risk of your hand being called dead."

Sherry paused, and then announced, "You know, I'm

thinking of going to the next drop-in session at the Club-house. What do you think?"

"Even if Lois is there?"

"*Especially* if she's there. She doesn't scare me anymore. I don't think I'll go up and ask Jerry to dance anytime soon, but I have just as much right to be in the Clubhouse as anyone else!" she declared.

"Good for you!" I said. "You're a lot more confident than when I first met you!"

"Thanks to you and, of course, to Franny and Carol. They're a hoot! I felt terrible that people think I intentionally hurt Fran," she said.

"I've heard all sorts of ridiculous stories since Mom moved in here," I said. "People are just looking for things to talk about."

"Sometimes the things they say are true. It's such a small community, you never know," she said. "My fling with Marty was over quickly, it was really more a flirtation than anything else. But I swear, with Jerry—there never was, and never will be, anything to talk about!"

In mid-December, after Sam Albert's rock-wall-climbing-and-IMAX birthday party, we invited Jodi to spend the night at our place. I knew it was going to be a noisy day and that she'd need to decompress. The next morning, while their kids were at Sunday School, Jodi's brother, Peter, and his wife, Nancy, came over for brunch—it would be just two couples and Jodi.

Right after our little jaunt down the Shore the previous month, I'd been confident that Jodi would speak to Carol, but nothing came of it. Nancy, Peter, and I arranged this event out of frustration. We agreed that we weren't staging an intervention with Jodi *per se*, but if the topic came up, then we would see how far we could take the conversation.

They arrived while Roger was picking up bagels. Jodi was still upstairs getting dressed, so the three of us had a little confab in the den. "Carol seems pretty strong to me," I said. "I think she's suspected for a long time that something was up, especially since that barbecue."

Peter sighed. "She keeps needling me, saying things like, 'Your sister's dying and no one will tell me,' or 'I know you know what's wrong, why aren't you saying anything?' I just feel like it's not for me to say. I have to respect Jodi's decision."

I agreed. "I don't want to go behind her back, either. In the end, it's got to come from Jodi."

Jodi and Roger joined us in the den. After a few jokes and some bagels, I said, "I heard you tell your mother that you had another migraine yesterday, to get out of the end of Sam's party."

"Of course. I've used that migraine excuse ever since high school. Whenever I didn't want to go out to dinner with the family, or if I wanted to stay home when Dad had tickets to a Nets game, it was, 'Oh, I've got a migraine.'" She grinned mischievously, proud of how easy it was to fool Carol. "Ma always bought it, or at least she told my dad not to bother me."

"Hmm," I mused. "Maybe she just thought you had your period and were calling it a migraine instead, trying to be polite."

Nancy looked at Jodi with a serious expression. "I'm going to say it, since no one else will. Your mother is worried. She knows something's changed, that your life is different. She's not a stupid woman."

Peter nodded. "She thinks it's something fatal, like a brain tumor or something. Or that you've got MS, like Aunt Dorothy. You need to talk to her."

Jodi was struck dumb momentarily. She scowled at me and said, "*Et tu, Brute?*" Then she turned to Peter, and unleashed more direct hostility.

"It's my life. Who are you to ambush me, after all I do for you, and tell me what I should and shouldn't say to Ma? I'm the older sister, I'm the one who helped raise you. Who are you to dictate?" Peter weathered her abuse, recognizing that she was actually just frustrated and, above all, scared.

She turned to Roger. "What do you think? Am I being cruel to a grieving widow by depriving her of something new to worry about?"

Roger cleared his throat. "Jodi, I don't know you well, but you're Talia's best friend so you're important to me too. I believe that you're generally an honest person, and you're definitely a practical person, so I'll keep this totally objective," he said, ever the scientist.

Something about his voice and rational demeanor calmed her. She nodded. "Go on."

"Your mother lost her husband a little more than a year ago. She has paid closer attention to your behavior since then—she might not have been as aware, two or three years ago, but now she sees the low energy, the avoidant behavior, the general secretiveness—she just went through a serious loss and she thinks she's about to do so again. She expects the worst."

I was pleased to see that Jodi was paying attention. Maybe Roger reminded her a little bit of Mike Belkin. She indicated that he should keep talking.

"My research is mainly in infectious diseases, not neurology. From what I've read, Chronic Fatigue Syndrome is unpredictable and sometimes temporarily debilitating, but if your symptoms are properly treated, it is not expected to shorten your life span.

"Your mother is under the impression that you have a fatal illness and that you're lying in order to cause her less pain. Bottom line: she's already worried, without knowing the facts. In this situation, the truth will most likely be a great relief to her. I think you should tell her." He folded his arms in an "I rest my case" pose. It struck me as funny: sometimes he and Abby were exactly alike.

"Okay, then," Jodi said. "Clarence Darrow here has convinced me. I didn't think she needed more health scares and aggravation," she sighed. "I thought I was making it easier for her."

"Maybe she couldn't be there for you when Dad was dying," said Peter, "but now she really believes that you're dying too. You'll be doing her a huge favor if you let her know what's going on."

"She'll want to help. It'll give her something constructive to do," Nancy added.

I had to speak up. "Is there more that you haven't told me, or Peter? Has Mike figured out anything new, and you're too embarrassed to tell anyone?"

"No, they know it's not anemia. He definitively ruled out Lyme and shingles a year ago. There are a few new tests he wants me to take next month, but my overall health has actually improved, thanks to my trainer. All my levels are better than when I stopped working—blood pressure, cholesterol, white blood cells."

"That's great news! Here's to your aggravating the rest of us for a long time to come!" said Nancy, raising her coffee mug.

Winter

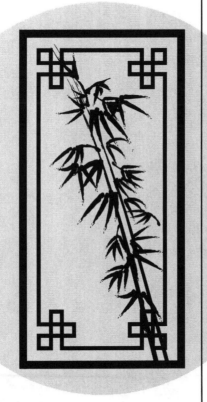

CHAPTER 33

Things stayed quiet in Parnassus Pines during the winter. I didn't teach a lot of mah jongg because so many residents became snowbirds in Florida. I also preferred to start with beginners in April, when the new card came out—no point in learning something that was just about to change.

I was able to give some extra time to my pet student, Sherry. Her foray into the Clubhouse card room had not been successful. Lois Benson controlled the crowd and made it obvious that she still didn't want her there. Mom and Carol weren't there to protect her and even if they had been, she really wasn't up to their speed of play. She needed to play with friendly people at her own level.

I had devised a great solution. I invited her to come over to my house one afternoon in late January, along with Janet and Annette, two of my more outgoing former students from Chestnut Arbor. It's so strange—people become connected in their own development and they rarely invite guests from other neighborhoods. I figured that the three of them would be able to have a good game together. Especially Janet—the one who had upset Ginger by leaving their little cruise group. She was a lot more independent-minded than most of her friends.

The afternoon was a big success. Annette and Sherry were at the same skill level, but it looked like Janet had been practicing a lot more. For instance, there was a situation where the Red Dragons she needed were exposed by someone else and she was able to change her hand. She ended up winning two games in a row.

"What have you been up to?" I asked her. "You weren't even looking at your card!"

Janet laughed. "I play online sometimes," she confessed. "I've found a few patient people and we arrange to go on around the same time. My friends are easy to play with, but some of those online players are so nasty!"

"You're right," I said. "I don't play online any more. I'm glad you met a few people that way, though. And you're so smart to schedule it!"

Sherry enjoyed the social aspect of our afternoon. When it was just the two of us playing in her apartment, it wasn't quite the same. You need four people to carry on all the crazy conversations that come up in a mah jongg game.

For instance, Annette threw out a Wind tile and said, "No-ath," with no "R" sound. We all laughed at the thick Brooklynese.

"You never seem to have an accent, except when you say that word!" said Janet. "Where did you grow up?"

"Midwood," she replied. "Are you girls from Brooklyn, too?"

"I'm from the Bronx," said Sherry. "What about you, Talia?"

"I was born in Manhattan, but my parents moved out here before my brother was born," I said. "Strictly a Jersey girl."

"Aha." As we mixed the tiles and set up the walls for the next game, the other ladies compared notes about accents and childhoods.

"A lot of Brooklyn people moved out to Long Island— I mean, Lawn Guyland," said Annette. "We came to New

Jersey, instead. My husband had a job with Johnson & Johnson."

"I was Harvey's office manager for many years. I've heard all kinds of accents," said Sherry. "I used to be able to tell which neighborhood people came from just based on the vowels!"

By the end of the afternoon, Janet had won about four dollars. I was up a dollar too. I'm sure that Sherry and Annette didn't mind losing; they'd had a wonderful time.

"Let's get together again!" said Annette. "Come over to see us at Chestnut Arbor, we'll find a fourth. You don't mind if we leave you out, Talia?"

"Not at all!" I said. "You girls don't need me!"

They exchanged cell numbers and email addresses, and Annette and Janet left. Sherry stayed behind to help me clean up the dishes and put away the tiles.

"They were really friendly," she told me. "It's great to meet people who don't already think they know everything about you!"

I laughed. "Yes, Parnassus Pines can get to be a little too close, I think. That's the trade-off of living in such a small community."

Sherry nodded. "There's a good side to it too. You know, Talia, I don't have much of a family. I wish I did. I think of you like a niece or something. I'm very fond of you, and look forward to our time together."

"I feel the same way," I told her.

"I'm usually pretty quiet," she admitted. "I don't always open up to people. Maybe it was the stories about the old neighborhood, but I just feel like talking, if that's all right.

Do you have time to chat?"

Suddenly I felt like a therapist. "What's on your mind?"

"You're going to think this is crazy," she said, "but remember my story about the Bronx Beach Club and meeting Harvey and the other boys?"

"Sure," I said. "You and…Peaches, right? You two were hanging out by the boys' locker room. It sounds like you had a great summer."

"And my story about working at the Concord as a photographer?"

"Yes, you were taking photos at the cocktail parties and selling them in the lobby later that weekend. I love your stories," I told her.

"Well, both those stories were about the same summer."

She enthusiastically told the story of how that summer began. She'd come up to the hotel in late May and was assigned to the photography staff. She was given a double room in the staff dorms behind the main hotel, partnered with one of the lifeguards from the children's pool.

They were about the same size, 4 Petite, so they were able to trade outfits. Since the roommate was in an official lifeguard bathing suit all day, Sherry could borrow her dresses for work—no one ever realized that they were sharing clothes.

Her first weekend working, she met a very sweet guy. He had come up with an older couple—husband and wife. She asked them if they'd like a family photo.

"Oh, they're not my parents," he said. "But of course, you should take a picture." She made sure to take a few of the trio during dinner on Friday evening, and again when there was dancing after the evening's entertainment. She saw them over the weekend, sitting together at the swimming pool, and again in the card lounge playing bridge with a second, older woman.

On Sunday morning, the young man came up to her booth in the lobby. When she asked about his companions, he told her that the couple was sleeping late. He explained that the older man had hired him for the summer. He was considering taking him on as a junior partner, and someday passing the business along to him.

She told him that the couple certainly seemed fond of him, and they talked seriously about what the upside would be of him inheriting the business, and whether it was the kind of thing he wanted to do with his life. He was the first real man she'd ever met. She usually dated high school and college boys, and all they wanted to talk about was sports, cars, or movies. He was actually asking her advice about an important life decision. "I still don't know why he trusted me." She shrugged at the memory.

The young man ended up ordering several of the enlargements. When he left that afternoon with the older couple, Sherry felt a pang of regret that they hadn't spent more time together. She had been very successful that weekend, selling fifty enlargements as well as hundreds of the little scopes. Her boss was pleased, and told her that she should focus on taking pictures of children during the week—"Weekends are for couples, weekdays are for families."

She kept herself busy, and was surprised the next Friday evening to find the same young man from the previous weekend smiling at her from the dining room singles table.

He'd come up alone this time, taking the smallest and cheapest room available, because he wanted to see her again.

There were a whirlwind few weekends. Her young man came up almost every weekend, sometimes with his boss and sometimes alone, always to spend as much time as he could with her. It was understood that she had to work. He would be waiting whenever she had a break: mostly right after lunch, and again during the nightclub show, when all eyes were on the main stage.

"He missed some great acts, like Steve Lawrence and Eydie Gorme, just to sit in the lobby!" she said. "He was very sweet, very thoughtful. And he never tried to go too far with me. It was an old-world courtship. He was several years older than me, but that didn't seem to faze him at all."

I told her it sounded like a wonderful romance. Obviously, I was waiting to hear about the conflict—something must have happened, or she would have married the guy.

She continued her story:

"Each Sunday evening, he would promise to return again the following Friday. I was looking forward to seeing him for the last weekend in July, but that Wednesday evening, after my day off, something terrible happened.

"My roommate was kind of a flirt, and occasionally brought guests back to our room while I was working or offsite. Around that time, a guest reported that some money and jewelry was missing, and it was found on my side of the room, hidden away in one of my drawers."

Sherry was accused of stealing. The chief of security didn't give her a chance to deny it. He said that the jewelry was found among her belongings and that was proof enough for

him. "We don't want a scandal, but you're lucky we aren't re-
porting you to the police. You're fired, effective immediately."

She had no chance to say goodbye to her beau, no chance
to talk to the roommate—Sherry was put on the next bus
back to the City. Of course, she was humiliated and afraid to
tell anyone back home what had happened. She explained it
away by telling her mother she was merely homesick.

"My first weekend back home, I went to the Beach Club
with Peaches. That's when I started spending time with Harvey and Jerry. I was still in shock, and not interested in
meeting anyone, but then these two guys were crazy about
me. At first, they were just a distraction. But Harvey really
was sweet."

"And what happened with your boyfriend?" I asked.

Sherry sighed. "I never spoke to him again."

CHAPTER

34

Jodi and I were back at Amici, having lunch. We'd both been craving their eggplant parm.

"Maybe the dead of winter isn't the best time to be house hunting, but I may as well start," she said. "I mean, I'll be out here during President's Week, anyway. I'm dogsitting for Peter."

"House hunting?" I asked. "You're going to move out to New Jersey?" I was ecstatic.

"Yeah. I haven't decided whether I'll tell Ma about the CFS before or after I tell her about the apartment. I'm not sure which will be a bigger surprise."

"She'll be thrilled. Is that a Valentine's Day present?"

"Kind of. I realized you guys were right. Ma's not getting any younger. She doesn't need to be worrying about whether she'll outlive me. It's a horrible thing, all this guilt." She looked at me and shook her head. "I didn't stand a chance against you, Roger, Mike, Nancy, Peter..."

"Where are they going for vacation?" I asked, trying to change the subject. "And why are you the designated pet sitter?"

"Peter and Nancy have an Ophthalmology Convention in Miami on the fifteenth, so they're going down for the whole week. They got a second hotel room for Ma so she can watch the kids all day while they go to meetings."

"So much fun!" I said sarcastically. "Too bad they didn't invite you to come too."

"All I have to do is watch Charles Barkley," she said. I looked at her, confused. "The dog, not the basketball player.

That's his name. Anyway, he's a lot easier to take care of than the two kids. I'm not complaining."

"When's the last time *you* took a vacation?" I asked her. "Was it before you were diagnosed?"

She stopped to consider the question. "I can't even remember. Gary and I never had time to travel much. The boyfriend before him...he liked to travel."

"Was he one of your ex-fiancés?" I asked. I was always looking for a chance to hear another story.

"Yes. That was Chris," she said.

"Chris? Was he Jewish?"

"Nope. Not in the least. Christopher Reckendorff. Lutheran. Adorable. Athletic, clever, a lot of fun."

"And you were engaged?" I asked.

"Yup. With a ring and everything."

"How long ago was this?" I continued the interrogation. "Come on, I want to hear more."

"Hmm. Must have been before I'd even met Gary. I guess I was in my late twenties. It was before the company launched." She was trying to remember. "I met him when one of my sorority sisters got married. He and I were both in the wedding party. That's always a great way to meet people," she added.

"So how long were you dating him before he proposed?"

"Only about eight months. It was pretty whirlwind. We went running together, liked the same things, never got into any fights. He brought me down to Virginia to meet his parents. He was easy to get along with. He didn't argue when I insisted our kids would have to be raised Jewish."

"So what was the problem?" I asked. "Why aren't you Jodi Reckendorff right now?"

She hesitated. "One night, we'd been out with a client of his, and Chris had too much wine. When we got home, he told me that he wasn't sure he'd be able to stay faithful to me."

"That's an impressive confession," I said. "At least he was honest with you."

"I appreciated the warning. He also mentioned that he was attracted to men, including that client."

"Oy!" I exclaimed. "*Really* honest of him. I guess it was all for the best that you ended it."

She nodded. "In a way, I lucked out. I can't imagine what would have happened if he had stayed sober that night. We were six months away from the wedding. We had some explaining to do—none of the private details, of course—but we got most of the deposits back on the reception. Chris is still in New York. We don't talk anymore, but I've seen him mentioned in the *Times*."

"Did he ever get married?" I asked.

"Yes, and divorced. He cheated on his husband too." She shook her head. "Some people aren't able to keep their vows, I guess."

———

Jodi's near-miss engagement story got me thinking about Uncle Fred and *his* failed marriage. Jodi had been able to call things off before they went too far. She'd been disappointed, of course, but nothing irreversible happened. She had returned the ring and moved on with her life. On the other hand, the whole youthful divorce episode had really taken its toll on Fred. According to my mother, he was married—and divorced—while I was still a baby, something like fifty years ago.

My curiosity had taken hold. The next time I was over at Mom's, I told her that I'd been wondering about Uncle Fred's short-lived marriage. "What happened? Was it a messy divorce?" I thought of Jodi. "Did she run off with another guy?"

"It was just a bad match," she shrugged. "He married a girl he barely knew and after a few months he regretted it. He asked for a divorce. She went down to Reno; it ended quickly."

"Who was she?" I asked.

"Just some girl he met on vacation. She was pretty, I guess, but we'd never even heard of her, and one day he came home—boom, 'I'm getting married.' My parents were shocked."

"Were they young? I mean, he must have been in his twenties by then." I was trying to get her to open up and tell more.

"It was the mid-sixties. You were already born, your brother wasn't alive yet. Fred was a young dentist—I *think* he was done with dental school…" She furrowed her brow. "I'm a little vague on some of the details."

"So he was in his twenties, a young dentist. He was a good dancer," I added. I was trying to lay out as much of the story as I could. "They met on vacation…"

"She was a rich girl. Spoiled. Awful. I don't know what he was thinking," she said. "He had dated lots of other girls when he was younger, but he was never serious about anybody."

It seemed like a youthful indiscretion. My mother mentioned that the girl was pretty. Maybe he just got overwhelmed with passion, swept up in a shipboard romance.

It definitely seemed out of character for Uncle Fred—Mom said he never had a serious girlfriend before her, and he certainly never had a serious one again after her, so what was it about this girl that got him to propose to her? Even if it hadn't worked out, there must have been a reason that he was willing to take that step.

Uncle Fred had shown himself to be a very sentimental person. It sounded like he believed in true love. Something must have gone horribly wrong for him to not want to stay with this girl. Then again, maybe it was only after the marriage *ended* that he became such a romantic. I wished I knew more of the details, but it seemed like asking him would only uncover old wounds. Better to leave him in peace.

After all the waiting and the guilt, it turned out to be rather anticlimactic when Jodi told Carol about her illness.

Peter and the family had just returned from Florida. Charles Barkley, their dog, was impossibly loud in his greetings. Carol saw that the noise was upsetting Jodi. "Want to come back to my place?" she asked.

They ended up on Carol's couch, watching old melodramas from the 1940s—Bette Davis, Barbara Stanwyck. "Lots of tough broads," Jodi explained.

Suddenly, it was all too much for her. When Fred MacMurray shot Barbara Stanwyck, Jodi started sobbing. "You know, Ma, everybody thinks I'm like that too."

Carol looked surprised. "How do you mean?"

"The company. When I ran it, all of my staff was afraid of me. No one thought I had a soft side. And now..."

Carol waited expectantly. "And now?"

"I'm sick, Ma. I'm not dying, but I'm sick. And I want to come back to New Jersey."

She told Carol all about the first few months, when she was afraid it was multiple sclerosis. She talked about not wanting to tell her parents while her father was dying, and how Mike Belkin had been such a help to her. She said that she hadn't even told *me* the truth until October.

Carol, of course, was very relieved. When my mother found out, she was initially upset that I hadn't told *her*, but I explained that it was up to Jodi and Carol to work out. The sad part was how little credit Roger got for convincing Jodi to come clean.

One immediate result was that Jodi no longer had to skulk around, pretending to lead a more exciting life than she did. She still didn't answer her phone in the evenings, but she wasn't lying to her mother about where she was or what she was doing.

Carol had reacted like I did, ever the nurturer. What books were there, where could she find out about CFS? She had started looking for support groups and reading articles about nutritional supplements. Just like me, Carol was happiest when she had a project, and now taking care of Jodi was her number one goal. This wasn't the way Jodi had wanted things to be—she liked her privacy and independence—but it was better for both of them to have the truth out in the open. Carol would have to learn to respect Jodi's space, and Jodi would have to let her mother help, in appropriate ways.

Jodi's plan to give up the New York City apartment could finally proceed. Paying higher taxes, commuting back and forth to spend time with the rest of us in New Jersey…none of it made any sense. The problem was still, where should she go instead?

"You could move in with us, now that the kids are both away at school," I said.

Jodi shook her head. "I really don't think Roger wants another woman around the house. Not a great set-up. Any other ideas?"

"You could hide away in the attic at Peter's. It would be like those gothic novels, the aunt that no one knows about…" I smirked.

"Oh, thanks. You are worse than no help. I really don't want to live with my mom. It's a small unit, and just too depressing to contemplate...she'd wake me every morning with a glass of orange juice, help me pack my book bag for school. No thanks. Let's talk about something else. How's your little project going?"

I had been giving Jodi updates about Sherry and her lessons, and told her about how well it went when the Chestnut Arbor ladies came over. I described how they'd been so friendly, laughing about Brooklyn and the Bronx and having a perfectly nice game.

"We had a lot of fun!" I said. "People who don't have some preconceived notion of Sherry think she's a great person. And she really is! It's just these ladies at the Pines. Thanks to Lois Benson, the mah jongg ladies all hate her. Maybe she should just move to Chestnut Arbor. She's more athletic, anyway."

"Good point. And I could take her unit." We both mulled that over for a moment. "You know," Jodi said, "it's not a half-bad idea. Let's see if she's interested. I could make it worth her while, I know C.A. is a little pricier..."

"It's too big, those homes are twice as big as the units at the Pines. It doesn't make sense," I said.

"Darn!" said Jodi. "It was worth a thought."

We talked about Benjy's life in the City. "He should move into my old place," she said.

"I think he has to be in the dorms for his first year. After that, he's got to find housing. You could sublet it to him in the fall...but it's not exactly a typical home for a college kid." Her apartment, in a luxury high-rise on East 62nd Street, was nowhere near his Greenwich Village campus.

"Benjy is no typical college kid," Jodi replied. "He'd make it look better than I did. You know, realtors would really hate my family. Mom gave her house up to Peter, and I could give my apartment to Benjy...no one's ever going to get a commission, the way this is going."

"I think you need to leave your apartment and be where you want to be—in New Jersey."

"Let's piece together this 'Sherry moves to Chestnut Arbor' thing. Maybe there's a guy there who's looking for a girlfriend?" she suggested.

"The official Divorced Guy at Chestnut Arbor? Another Marty situation? No way, let's not put Sherry through that again."

CHAPTER 36

A few days later, I had an unexpected errand to run. My mother needed some complicated dental work—she'd cracked a tooth and had to get a new crown. She insisted that she wouldn't go to anyone but Uncle Fred, and asked me to drive her to Westchester. We headed up to Mount Kisco first thing on Thursday morning. Fred made an arrangement with the young partner who had taken over his practice; he was using one of the rooms, and had a dental assistant lined up, just for the day.

"I really appreciate this," my mother said. "I know what a hassle it is for you."

"Actually, I enjoy it," he confessed. "I still carry insurance so that I can see special patients like you. I just don't want the day-to-day obligation anymore."

He turned to me. "Why don't you make yourself comfortable in my private office, Talia? We're all going to be here for a while."

I wanted to peek at the waiting room first. Fred was right. The younger dentist had changed things up a bit, expanding the pediatric dentistry angle with new decor. There was an interactive screen for kids and several alcoves with creative decorations: a castle, a deep-sea scene, a circus. It was a lot more fun than the boring *Highlights* magazines he had when I was a kid.

I walked into Fred's private office, full of textbooks and old mementos from patients. He'd had a good, long run in that practice. He came in to talk to me while Mom was getting numb with the novocaine.

"I like what your partner did with the waiting room," I told him. "It's cute. The practice is evolving."

"Sure, that's what happens when you pass it on. I remember when Dr. Shenker passed it down to me. I was his partner for almost ten years before he decided to retire. Nice guy," he added.

"Was he interested in a family practice too?"

"No, he didn't have kids in here at all. I first had the idea of treating children when you were little. Your mother needed somewhere to take you and Steven, and was willing to come all the way up here because she trusts me. I had to buy some specialized equipment."

"Was he still your partner then?"

"Yep. That was probably about five years in. It took me that long to convince him to add on the pediatric part."

"That's sweet," I said. "I like that the practice has been handed down from him, to you, and now to Dr. Brinkman. And it's good that it keeps changing."

He nodded. "Shenker was a good man. Treated me like a son." He gestured over to a picture on the wall. "I have to get back to Fran. The novocaine should be working by now."

After he left, I glanced at the photo that he'd indicated. Hanging among his diplomas and certificates, it was a picture of a very young Uncle Fred in a white dinner jacket and black cummerbund. He was standing, smiling, between two people also dressed in summer-weight formal wear. These must have been Dr. and Mrs. Shenker. It took me a moment to notice the words printed in gold on the bottom right: "Concord Hotel, 1965."

Suddenly, my head was spinning. It didn't seem possible. It was probably all just a funny coincidence, but my gut instinct was telling me that I should keep pursuing my line of thought.

I retraced all the facts. Sherry had said that she met Harvey in August 1965. Another time, she told me about the job she had held, earlier in the same summer. She'd worked as a photographer, taking pictures of the guests at the Concord Hotel. She also told me that before she got fired, she'd met someone really special: a young man who was hosted by his boss and the boss's wife.

And here was Uncle Fred, in a photo with *his* boss and boss's wife, taken at the Concord Hotel during the summer of 1965. It was certainly possible that Sherry took this picture. It was considerably less possible that Fred was Sherry's young man. Still, what were the odds of them having crossed paths fifty years ago? I wanted to know more about the story.

Uncle Fred was still down the hall, working on my mother's crown. I heard their lopsided conversation. As he worked, he kept asking questions about Benjy and Abby and my mother grunted monosyllables in reply. I heard him tell her, "This is going to have to set for about ten minutes. I'll be back," and he started walking back to his private office.

There were so many questions I could have asked. "*Do you remember the girl who took this picture? Were you in love with her? When did you meet your wife? What the heck happened during the summer of 1965?!*" I had to think fast.

I realized that Uncle Fred didn't even know that I knew that he'd been married. It would have been pretty awkward for me to suddenly ask him about his romantic history, out of the blue. I searched my mind for something that would support my theory, but wouldn't upset Uncle Fred. *Ah, yes.*

"That's a great picture," I said. "You know, Mom and Dad took us to the Concord Hotel back when we were little kids. Did you go up there often?"

"Oh—I forgot that that's written on the photo. Funny. Yes, I spent several weekends there when I was younger. It used to be a pretty big deal, very popular. They got some great acts up there. Real headliners, like Steve and Eydie, dance teams, comedians."

"Did you go there to play golf?" I asked, fishing for information. "I hear they had a great course."

"No, I was invited up there by the Shenkers. They wanted to get to know me better. I played a little bridge, went to the shows. I wasn't so athletic, back then."

I nodded. *Bridge with the Shenkers and a second, older woman.* I wanted to say, "Tell me about the photographer!" but I thought better of it. *Don't blow your cover, don't upset him. Just let the truth come out over time.*

"The Shenkers kept inviting you? That was really nice of them," I prodded.

"Two or three times. Sometimes I went up on my own." *Yes. Yes, you did.*

"Too bad there aren't hotels like that anymore," I said. "I mean, Abby met Ethan through school, of course, but there should be more areas for young people to meet up in the summer. It sounds like it was quite a romantic place."

He gave me a funny look. "Yes, it was considered a big resort for singles. Families too, though," he added. "I'm going to see how your mother's doing."

I heard him mumbling quietly to my mother. She gave a questioning grunt; then a "hmm, interesting" grunt; another, more complacent "okay" grunt; and finally an "I don't know" grunt. It was hard to interpret the entire conversation from her inflections. I couldn't wait to hear her take on their discussion during the long car ride home.

"You're going to want to take some ibuprofen tonight, Franny," he said, as we walked out of the building together. "And try not to eat anything too hot or cold for the rest of the day."

He opened my mom's car door and kissed her on the cheek. "It's been a pleasure," he said. He came around to the driver's side and gave me a hug.

"I'll see you soon, I hope," I told him. "Thanks for taking good care of Mom."

———

The minute we drove off, I began barraging her with questions. "What was he asking you?" I said.

"When?"

"When he came back in, at the end of the procedure."

"He just wanted to see if it hurt and if I could feel any unevenness," she explained.

"Really?"

I was disappointed. I'd been hoping that he was asking her how I knew so much about his past, and telling her what a fantastic detective I must be.

"He's a dentist, Talia. That's what he *does.*" She sighed. "What were *you* asking *him*?"

"Why?" I asked.

"He seemed a little rattled," she said. "Distracted. What were you talking about?"

"Eh, just hotels and stuff," I said. "Do you remember anything else about how he met his wife?"

"Oh, you didn't!" she said. "Did you ask him about Lorraine?"

"Who's Lorraine?" I asked.

"His ex-wife. That's true, I guess I never mentioned her name."

"No, you didn't," I said. "And I didn't ask him about her, exactly. I just talked about the Concord. Is that where they met?"

"Yes, up in the Catskills. He met her and within a few weeks they were engaged. It was lunacy."

"Please tell me what you remember," I begged. "She was pretty, she was spoiled. It ended quickly. You don't even have photos, because they got divorced so fast. What else?"

"She had a brother. Oh, what a jerk. His name was Ronald. At the wedding, he kept trying to get me alone in a corner. I was a married woman! And a young mother! What kind of a…" She was still infuriated. "Horrible family. I'm forever grateful that they ended it quickly. I can't imagine what I might say or do if I ever had to see those people again."

CHAPTER 38

I was in hot pursuit, now, but I wanted to get someone else's opinion. After I dropped off my mother, I called up Jodi and said, "I've got a great puzzle for you. When are you free?"

"I was planning to come out to New Jersey on Saturday. Can you wait two days?"

"Sure," I said. "Stop by for lunch. Bring your mom."

I called Sherry too, and asked if I could see her on Friday. "Let's just get together for coffee, we don't have to play mah jongg," I told her.

"Okay, I'll be done with tennis at around two. Come by then."

"Great," I said.

I made one final call, to my mother. "How are you feeling? Is the medicine helping?"

"Yes, thanks for asking," she said. "Listen, please don't talk about the past with Uncle Fred. He seemed really upset."

"Can I ask *you* a question, then?"

"Okay…"

"Did he ever say why he got married right away, or why he ended it so quickly?"

"No," she said. "I really have no idea why it ended, except for the fact that she was perfectly vile. Oh yes, I meant to tell you. I found the wedding announcement. I told you, there weren't any photos or even invitations, it happened so fast. The event itself was very small, but her parents printed up cards and sent them out afterward. I think they were hoping for more gifts."

"Hmm. Can I look at it?"

"Sure, come by in the morning. I'm going to bed now. I took an extra ibuprofen, I hope I can sleep this off." She yawned. "Your Uncle Fred does good work, but no one can do this stuff painlessly."

———

I stopped by Mom's house on Friday morning with some yogurt. She was still in her bathrobe.

"How is it going this morning? Are you still on soft food?"

"I'm mostly having liquids, but thank you. Here, I wanted to show you." She pulled out a small card.

Aaron and Mabel Haskell
wish to share the joyous news
of the marriage of their daughter
Lorraine Eleanor
to
Dr. Frederick Geliebter
on the second of October, 1965

"That was quick," I said. "Only two months."

My mother looked confused. "What?"

"Oh, I meant it must have been pretty fast. You said they met during the summer, and here it was only early October when they got married." I realized she'd never actually said how long Fred knew Lorraine, but if I was right, then he was the man who'd promised to come back and visit Sherry at the end of July.

"Can I hold on to this for a few days?" I asked.

My mother looked at me quizzically. "I know you're up to something. Please don't say you've found Lorraine, and do not go looking for her. *Please.*"

"I swear, I have not found Lorraine," I said. "Don't worry."

———

At two o'clock, I was sitting in Sherry's condo, ready to get some facts. She only had said nice things about the young man who may or may not have been my Uncle Fred. I felt pretty confident that whatever we discussed would satisfy my curiosity.

"How was your tennis game?" I asked her.

"We creamed them." She grinned. "Marge is a great partner. Most people think she's tough, but they underestimate *me* because I'm so small. It's very funny when they challenge me at net."

"Good for you!" I said. "Sounds like you're a fierce competitor."

"When I need to be," she said.

"I bet you catch them off guard. So, tell me, did you ever fight over a guy?"

"What, with Peaches? No, she always liked a different type than I did. There was only one time that another girl tried to steal my boyfriend."

"Someone was flirting with Harvey?" I asked, hoping that wasn't what she meant.

"Actually, it was a girl up at the Concord Hotel. This awful girl and her brother were always bothering me and my boyfriend. The brother, Ronald, would try to distract me so that she could spend more time with my guy. Ronald was such a creep."

"Oh, really?" I asked. I wanted to add: *My mother thought so too.*

"I guess she won, in the end. He ended up marrying her."

"The one who kept trying to take him away?" I asked. "Ronald's sister?"

"That's the one," she said. "They sent me a wedding announcement and it made me really upset. I got it the day before Jerry and Harvey had the basketball game, and Harvey's nose got broken."

"Their basketball duel was the day after you heard about the wedding?"

"Yes. I still can't believe how quickly they got married. He must have liked her more than I thought."

"Maybe he was just ready to get married," I said. I reminded her, "You got engaged two weeks later too."

"That's true," she said. "Poor Harvey, I felt so bad for him."

Did you feel bad about losing Fred too? I wondered.

"Tsk. Playing those games, fighting over people," she mused. "Jerry broke Harvey's nose. That girl, Lorraine—"

"Lorraine. Hmm," I said, trying not to betray any emotion.

"Lorraine constantly maneuvering to get my boyfriend alone. I have to say, all that *mishegos*, I'm glad that's over with. The problems about Marty were a real headache too. You know, it's a relief to know I'll never fall in love again. It's not worth the aggravation."

"Were you in love with Marty?" I asked in disbelief.

"Oh Lord, no. He was just keeping me company. Courteous, helpful, but such a dope. He makes Jerry Benson look like a brilliant conversationalist. No, I haven't been in love in many, many years. Harvey and I were happy together, and he was good to me, but it wasn't like lightning struck, not like that first time in the Catskills. When I heard he was married, it just broke my heart."

I felt sympathy for poor Harvey. He was kind and patient for almost fifty years. I'm sure Sherry treated him well, and a marriage doesn't have to be the paragon of romance, but still it was sad to hear she felt that way. On the other hand...

"I'm glad you're still competitive on the tennis court!" I said. "And you're still very pretty. You never know who'll cross your path."

"I'm really not interested in meeting anyone," she said. "Really."

CHAPTER 39

I had collected all the pieces of the puzzle and couldn't wait to share them with Jodi and Carol, but to what end? Sherry had said she had no interest in meeting anyone. Maybe she'd make this one exception?

When motivated, I can be quite the overachiever. By the time the Alberts showed up on Saturday morning, I had assembled charts, maps, and timelines and laid them out on the dining room table. I wanted to present a solid case.

"What is all this? A new project?" Carol asked.

"Sit down, sit down," I said, all excited. I looked at Jodi. "You know how our mothers set us up as friends?"

"Yeah?" Jodi asked. She glanced over to see Carol grinning smugly. "Listen, Ma, even a broken clock is right twice a day." She turned back to me. "What's your point?"

"I'm kind of a matchmaker too," I gushed. "This has been brewing since August or so. Wait until you hear this."

I laid out the story as best I could, using all my visual aids and listing the various characters. Afterward, I let my audience go over the facts.

Jodi recounted: "So Sherry didn't steal Jerry from Mah Jongg Lois Benson, because she knew him first. Jerry and Harvey were best friends. They had a basketball match to see who got Sherry—and Jerry won the match, 11-2, and broke Harvey's nose. Sherry felt so bad that she got engaged to Harvey, but both of them were a consolation prize, because she was still in love with..."

220

"Your Uncle Fred," Carol chimed in. "Whom she met up at that hotel, but never saw again because she got fired for stealing jewelry. I bet she was framed by that brother and sister."

"Ronald and Lorraine," I prompted.

"And Lorraine coincidentally married your Uncle Fred..."

"Only two months after Sherry was sent away," I said.

"The plot thickens," Jodi murmured.

"The plot was already pretty damned thick," said Carol. "Oy. Poor Sherry. Did you ever meet this Lorraine? Can we prove whether she and Ronald framed Sherry to get her out of the way?"

"It looks conclusive to me," I said. "I'm not a lawyer or anything, but it doesn't matter. There's no way to fix that part now."

I heard voices coming from the kitchen. Abby and Ethan were home for the weekend, and had just come back from the bagel store. When they heard the word "lawyer," their ears must have perked up. They walked into the dining room to observe the evidentiary proceedings. To bring them up to speed, I started over from the beginning, complete with visual aids.

When I was finished, Ethan applauded.

"*How* long did Uncle Fred's marriage last?" Abby asked.

"Six months," I said. "She went to Reno for a divorce."

"Wow. I'd love to hear that story," she said. I explained to Abby that my mother had forbidden me from asking Uncle Fred about it. I also told her about some of the surprisingly sentimental things that he had said at Benjy's graduation barbecue.

Everyone was pondering the situation in their own way, trying to piece the whole story together. I was glad I finally had some company to share it with and was hoping for some validation.

"Fred didn't stay married to Lorraine because he didn't love her," Carol announced. "He's a hopeless romantic and he's still in love with Sherry. I know it."

"What makes you so sure, Ma?" Jodi asked.

Carol turned and explained to Jodi: "Fred's private office sounds a lot like your father's. Daddy only kept his most treasured things there." She looked at me. "There must have been dozens of pictures taken of Fred and Dr. Shenker, but the one that he kept up in his office all these years…"

"Was the one that Sherry took the night they met! Oh my goodness." I had goosebumps.

"What are we going to do?" asked Jodi.

"We need an excuse to get them together," said Carol.

"How about an engagement party?" asked Ethan.

Even though we threw the whole thing together quickly, Ethan and Abby's engagement party turned out to be a great success. They were happy, and my mother and Roger's parents were thrilled to be sharing the moment with Ethan's extended family.

"They're going to produce the most adorable babies!" said Ethan's mother. I wholeheartedly agreed.

Abby responded with a lecture. "I don't see myself becoming a parent in the next three to five years, but regardless, I refuse to allow my role as a mother to define my professional career. If and when we decide to have children, Ethan will be playing an equal role in childrearing. We're doing background research now, and we will only be interviewing with companies and law firms that offer strong parental leave benefits."

Ethan just smiled and went along with whatever she said. He's such an astute young man.

I got to play a role in one of the best parts of the evening. It took place in our kitchen. Sherry was asked to come over early to help me set up for the party. Carol and I had decided that it would not be fair to blindside her, so I tried to be as gentle as possible.

We were arranging a fruit platter with dipping sauce. "I know you said you're not interested in meeting anyone," I said, "but would it be all right if we *reintroduce* you to an old friend?"

She looked at me with a curious expression. "What do you mean?" she asked.

I stepped back for a second, trying to phrase things delicately. "We still haven't talked that much about your younger days. For instance, I don't know your maiden name."

"It's Hartzig," she said. She was still puzzled. "Why?"

"My mom's is kind of Old World too," I said, "but I think you've heard it before: Geliebter?"

She let out a small cry of recognition. "I…I do know that name," she said, blushing. "Is he coming tonight?"

I nodded. "You can back out now, if you want. He doesn't know that you'll be here."

"Is there still…is *she* coming over too?"

I laughed. "Lorraine? No, she won't be here. Their marriage didn't last long enough for the ink to dry on the marriage certificate."

She covered her mouth with her hand. "I've got to get ready," she told me, and fled to the powder room.

Just then, Roger called me out of the kitchen to introduce me to Ethan's grandmother and great-aunt, who had flown in from Arizona. A few minutes later, Uncle Fred arrived. We introduced him to Ethan's parents and sister, his grandparents, the great-aunt, his uncle and aunt from Rochester, and his cousin from Manhattan.

Finally, I was able to pull Uncle Fred aside. "There's someone else who's been waiting to see you for quite a while," I announced.

He looked at me, slightly bewildered.

"Just go," I said, and pushed him downstairs to the den.

As much as it pained me not to watch, I had other important things to do as mother of the bride-to-be. I returned to my hostess duties. Of course, I was excited to meet Ethan's family, but I was also dying to know whether my matchmaking plan was successful.

———

I heard everything, after the fact:

Sherry told me, "I paced back and forth downstairs for about twenty minutes, waiting for Fred to show up. As far as I knew, he still thought I was some kind of criminal—that is, if he remembered me at all. I was terrified, but I had to see him again, if only to clear my name."

When Fred came downstairs, he didn't know quite what he would find. "You were very mysterious, Talia," he said, "pushing me down the stairs. I wasn't expecting…well, I've been fixed up with dozens of women over the years. Whenever people tell me they want me to meet someone, or 'someone's waiting for you,' or whatever, it's never been the person that I wanted to see. Until that moment."

They were both beaming at me, sitting across the table, holding hands like teenagers.

"I couldn't believe it," Fred continued. "She looked as beautiful to me as the last time I'd seen her. I didn't know how she got there, though!"

"I explained that you were my friend, and that somehow, you'd put together that we'd met at the Concord. I never dreamed that telling you all those stories would bring him back to me," she added.

"I'm a sucker for a good story," I told them, "and I like solving puzzles. I didn't even know Uncle Fred had been married, until this past summer."

Fred and Sherry had shared their stories that first night,

but they told them again for my benefit:

"When I got to the Concord that weekend, I naturally went looking for Sherry. Some of her fellow photographers told me that she had been fired. Her supervisor said that Sherry had fooled and betrayed the entire community. I was stunned.

"Lorraine made a beeline for me and attempted to 'console' me. The Shenkers invited her to join us for a drink—to them, she seemed perfectly sweet, and they could see that I was a wreck. She insinuated herself quickly into our group. Before I knew it, we were alone in the moonlight, and Lorraine made her feelings clear. She threw herself at me and said she'd been in love with me for weeks. She never left my side for a second. By the next weekend, she'd pressured me into buying a ring and setting a date. It all moved very quickly, steered assuredly by Lorraine."

"Meanwhile," Sherry explained, "I was down in the Bronx, being wooed by Harvey and Jerry. It wasn't working in the slightest—I was miserable and embarrassed, and didn't think of either of them romantically. It was just a way to spend time, although Harvey did have his amusing moments. When I got the wedding announcement, I gave up all hope. When Harvey and Jerry came over the next day, I decided that perhaps I needed to move on with my life."

"I didn't know it at the time," said Fred, "but Lorraine must have tracked down Sherry's address through the Concord staff. She sent the wedding announcement to Sherry as a victory gesture." But even as Sherry was learning about the marriage, it was unravelling rapidly. "We had very little in common, and Lorraine spent all our money, shopping every day while I worked at Dr. Shenker's office.

"One night, Lorraine got very drunk and bragged about how she and her brother, Ronald, had successfully framed Sherry. Ronald had hidden some of Lorraine's bracelets and necklaces in Sherry's drawer while he was visiting her roommate, and then Lorraine went to the Chief of Security, complaining that her jewelry was missing.

"I was shocked when I realized how I'd been duped. It was the final straw. I couldn't live with such a person. I wanted a divorce, as quickly as possible, and paid for Lorraine to go down to Reno."

The divorce became final on April twenty-sixth. That same day, Fred read about the April twenty-fourth wedding of Sherry Hartzig and Harvey Kandel. "I decided the best thing would be to let her have a happy life—there had already been enough disruption."

Sherry said, "We did have a successful marriage. Harvey was good to me. I never looked for Fred; I was still embarrassed about being fired, and assumed that he'd sent me the wedding announcement to tell me not to bother him. Even so, I was shocked that he would settle for someone as awful as Lorraine. I knew she wasn't worthy of him."

She summed it up: "Telling you those stories about the Concord made me think about all his wonderful qualities. I allowed myself to miss him, for the first time in years. When you told me your mother's maiden name, I was terrified. But when you said Fred was divorced, I suddenly had hope."

Abby called me a week later, when she was back at school. "Ethan and I were curious, so we went on LexisNexis to search for information about Lorraine and her brother. We just wanted to know what happened to them."

"Did you find anything?" I asked.

"Court records, articles from the *New York Post*. You won't believe it. Apparently, there was a double murder trial back in 1974, *New York State v. Eric 'Scoops' Newland*. Scoops was a crime boss from Long Island. He had a party in his home, and Ronald and Lorraine Haskell were there. Newland's girlfriend, Linda Sugarman, claimed that Ronald sexually assaulted her, so some of Newland's associates invited Ronald to take a little ride with them. Lorraine insisted on going, as well."

"Incredible," I said. "So what happened?"

"Scoops was declared not guilty. The Haskells' bodies were never found."

Epilogue

A s I said at a *different* engagement party, a month later: "My Uncle Fred is a deeply romantic man. Except for a small misstep, he remained steadfastly faithful to the girl he fell madly in love with fifty years ago. My mother was fortunate to spend twenty-two years with her true love; I can only hope that Fred and Sherry will have at least that long together."

The wedding was a lovely, small event. For old time's sake, and because Harvey would have wanted her to do it, Sherry invited the Bensons. None of us was accustomed to seeing Lois with such a wide grin on her face.

When they returned from their extended honeymoon, the newlyweds moved into Chestnut Arbor, where Sherry has become active on the Seniors' tennis team. Her Parnassus Pines unit currently is being sublet by Jodi, but next winter, the Albert women will spend January through March in West Palm Beach, Florida, as they scout for the three- or four-bedroom unit that will become their "winter palace." Benjy is living in New York City, a place where Abby and Ethan will *never* reside.

From April through December, I expect to have a weekly mah jongg foursome including Carol, my mother, and my Aunt Sherry. Jodi still says that she doesn't want to learn how to play, but she's happy to join us for conversation and snacks…and that's just fine with me.

Acknowledgments

I would like to thank a few special individuals:

Jen Gordon, founder of *Mad About Mah Jongg* and Mahj Mistress of Wausau, Wisconsin, who believed in me and launched a new phase of my writing career.

Johni Levene, founder of *Mah Jongg, That's It!* and Tile Queen of Los Angeles, who gave me encouragement and the opportunity to connect with literally thousands of other players.

Alice Sadaka and **Shelby Rhyne**, my official Booster Squad from the moment they read *Searching for Bubbe Fischer*. Everyone needs friends like you two.

Alice Shelton, the first person beyond *my* small world who actually invited me to come speak.

Tracy Taylor Callard, my voice of reason and the source of many a good story.

Maureen Komisar Luddy, who proved that fairy tales can come true.

Audrey Glick, Ricki Wovsaniker, Elisa Hirsch, Shari Gooen, and **Amy Gooen**, *Small World*'s steadfast readers, editors, and critics. I should note that the three ladies who are related to me—by marriage—don't even play mahj. That's how dedicated they were to the project.

Duane Stapp and **Ruth Mullen**, who continue to add the perfect style and polish to my books.

Marti Leimbach, who encouraged me to pursue fiction. It's nice to know I'm not the only person who likes to disappear into another world, even if it's only in my head.

Carlyn Liberman Altman and **Donna Shapiro Castillo** and their mothers—once I got approval from those ladies, I knew I was on the right track.

The original **Mrs. Gooens**, **Sue** and **Rita**, for their constant support and pride in my projects.

My mom, **Ellen Levy**, a Mahj Civilian who loves every word I write.

My students and mahj companions, none of whom bear any resemblance to these characters.

My daughters, who are both amazed and amused that "Mom found something to do" when they went away to college.

And my husband, **Michael**, without whom none of this would be possible.

Is your group or organization looking for a fun program?

I'm available to lecture about all aspects of mah jongg: etiquette, rules, strategy, history, or the psychological benefits of the game.

Contact me at *bubbefischer@gmail.com*